When I'm Bad I'm Better

When I'm Bad I'm Better

K.F. Johnson

One Ironwoman Publishing

Contents

Contents

One Ironwoman Publishing
Grayson, GA 30017

Cover Art: Christine N. Davis
ISBN: 978-1-954469-02-0

Valerie

Whoever said 'keep your friends close and your enemies' closer' obviously forgot to factor relatives into the equation. Sometimes, family breeds more snakes inside your house than there are outside of it. It's those same blood ties and family obligations that sometimes force you to deal with people that you otherwise wouldn't spit on if they were on fire.

Now, as I stood paralyzed gawking at the people before me with tears flooding my eyes...I wished I had a match.

My fiancé's muscular body glistened with the sheen of sweat as he knelt naked on the king size bed with his back to me and his face firmly planted between the legs of a hip bucking bitch. They were oblivious to my presence while The Dream's song "Fruition" blared from the surround sound speakers providing theme music for their betrayal. Her legs dangled over his shoulders as he eagerly devoured her, and pleasure filled moans escaped her cooing lips.

"Oh yeees!" she squealed as the rage rose in my chest compelling me to stop spectating and take action instead.

I kicked off one stiletto and grasped the other in my hand as I approached with my heart palpitating so hard, I could almost hear it. Pouncing on them, I wielded my heel in a frenzy like Jack the Ripper with a knife. He howled jerking upwards in a half turn and frantically defended himself trying to swat and grab my weapon. The eyes of the familiar female popped open like a jack in the box as she confusedly scurried backwards towards the headboard trying to avoid my blows. I continued to draw blood striking his back, shoulders and any exposed flesh I could reach as he fended me off.

"You sneaky-mother-fucker's!" I screeched wounding Brent in the hand and arm before he snatched the shoe and shoved me roughly backwards onto the carpet.

"What the fuck are you doing? Calm down God damn it!" he yelled angrily throwing my shoe across the room while her juices still dampened his lips.

"Fuck you Brent!" I spat feeling an ache in my ass far less painful than the one in my heart.

His broad chest visibly rose and fell with each breath and his muscular legs were firmly planted in a defensive stance as blood trickled from his wounds. His dark eyebrows furrowed in confusion as every muscle in his coffee brown face tensed. Flickers of guilt slowly invaded his almond shaped eyes which worriedly darted from her to me.

"Oh, don't look confused now nigga!" I hissed.

His accomplice cautiously watched me while dismounting the bed and approaching a garment on the floor. Surprisingly, she didn't look embarrassed or remorseful at all. In fact, the bitch looked annoyed.

Scrambling to my feet I charged her throwing a punch that connected with her cheek just as she was about to say something, but not before she shot a hand out catching me in the face. I swung back again but she blocked it with her forearm. She was fast. But not fast enough to stop the fiya I tried to smack out of her with my left hand when it landed against her face. She stumbled backwards bouncing off of the bed and then rushed towards me like a bull trapped in an arena.

We went at it, punching, slapping and pulling at each other while screaming obscenities. I was giving as good as I got at first. But then she uppercut me knocking me backwards and quickly grabbed hold of my hair, viciously jolting me forward in mid-motion. I went down hard on one knee and dizzily reached up to pry her grip from my mane. Suddenly my ears were ringing as a barrage of punches landed all over my head and face. I tried to block her blows with my hands and rip out tracks of her weave, but she was relentless.

"You-fucking-stuck-up-bitch," she taunted through gritted teeth dragging me forward with one hand wrapped around my locks.

"Get off of me!" I screamed swinging blindly as she shoved my head downward continuing to punish me.

Damn, I hadn't had a fight since the 5th grade and my lack of skill showed against this heffa who I already knew didn't hesitate to fight at the drop of a hat. I was clearly losing. My face and scalp ached as hair follicles were ripped from it and my knees burnt from the carpet she dragged me across. I felt Brent's arm around my waist pulling me while shouting for us to break it up and trying to pry her fingers from my hair.

"Naw! Naw! Don't save the hoe! She came at me like she was gonna beat my ass so let her fight!" she yelled delivering one last jab to my face before letting go and allowing him to pull me away.

When I steadied myself, I angrily snatched away from him, punching him in the chest a few times as I did. Huffing and puffing, I glared daggers at both of them through my mussed hair and aching face. She stared back at me with balled fists and an equal ferocity, breathing heavily through her flaring nostrils as tears lined her lashes.

"What the fuck are you crying for you backstabbing bitch! You're the one in here with my man's face in between your legs!" I spat at her sniffling away my own tears and holding my right eye which was throbbing like somebody was in my face knocking to get out.

It was almost hard for me to speak with the ball of emotions lumping in my throat. To add insult to injury, Musiq Soulchild's song "Love" began playing through the speakers as I dabbed the blood from my bottom lip with my tongue. That was the song Brent and I were going to use as our wedding march.

"I'm crying because I'm mad!" She defended jabbing an accusing finger in the air while her pierced nipples shook angrily with her breasts in agreement. "Fucking stabbing people with shoes and shit like some kind of psycho," she protested touching her bleeding left calve where I'd apparently nicked her.

"You're mad? Bitch please! You're trifling is what you are!" I hollered through tears turning towards Brent. "And of all of the bitches you could've cheated on me with you had to choose my twin sister?"

Brent ran his hands over his face and let his palms rest over his mouth as his eyes searched everywhere except my face for answers.

"I didn't plan to," he mumbled pitifully rubbing his chin.

His gaze was downcast, but then, as if noticing me for the first time, he surveyed me from bottom to top, registering the black strappy lace teddy with elongated cut outs on the sides and the sheer thigh high stockings I was wearing. I felt one of the stockings hanging down by my ankles, so I knew the disheveled hot mess I probably looked like now was a far cry from how I'd arrived.

His dismal expression met my distraught one. There's nothing more humiliating than showing up in lingerie to surprise your fiancé with a hot sexcapade and being surprised yourself that he was already having one. Well, nothing other than getting beat up by the side bitch who's also your twin sister that is.

"It just...happened," he offered contritely clasping his hands atop his bald head and swaying.

I turned to Vanessa who was also watching him with a blank expression and cut my eyes at her. People claim we resemble Logan Browning, the girl that plays the mean chick Jelena on the TV show Hit The Floor, but without makeup, I didn't think so. Like her, we're 5'3", have high cheek bones, cat like hazel eyes, caramel complexions and naturally brown hair that hangs just past our shoulders. Well, Vanessa's lengthened hers with clip-ins to reach the small of her back.

Like Logan's character though, I'm also a professional dancer with a petite and toned body to show for it, except I dance for the Alvin Ailey Dance Company of Atlanta instead of for a basketball team. Vanessa is a freelance makeup artist and apparently a part time backstabbing hoE. We haven't had the close bond most identical twins brag about since we were kids and we've definitely had our share of sibling rivalry issues, but this...was too much.

"Listen, Val, if it wasn't me...it would've just been somebody else. What did you expect him to do when you're putting your career before him and rationing out the pussy? Shit, you was barely even giving the man head," she chastised crooking her neck with a hand on her hip. "I tried to tell you a man like him don't want no prude; but your goody-two-shoes ass can't see that. All that good girl shit might impress everybody else, but a man...a real man...wants a freak in the bed. Not Mary Poppins," Vanessa continued smugly sweeping her hair over her shoulders while seizing her yellow maxi dress from the floor.

I glared at my doppelganger as she slid the dress over her head and spied Brent in my peripheral making facial expressions that said he wished she'd shut up. My head was swimming with feelings of anger and hurt in addition to the effects of the numerous blows, courtesy of my sibling.

"So, you had to be the one to prove it to me? Aren't you juggling enough dicks already without adding my man's to the mix? You've always been such a jealous, selfish, bitch. What is wrong with you? I'm your sister for Christ's sake. So what you think is gonna happen now? Are you supposed to replace me and live happily ever after together?" I blew out a sarcastic breath. "Good luck with that."

She cackled and wiped her damp face with the heels of her hands while Brent slid on his boxers.

"Jealous? Girl pu-lease. Jealous of what? You don't have anything I want that I can't have. Need proof? Did you just walk in on your man eating my pussy...or was it the other way around?" she taunted lifting her dress and patting her bare vagina. "Upgrade. Downgrade," she stated pointing a thumb at herself first and then a finger at me.

I wanted to scratch that superior expression right off of her face, but wasn't stupid enough to solicit a second beat down. I wiped the tears and caked on makeup I'd spent an hour applying to look glamorous for Brent from my face and glared at the man we were fighting over.

"How could you do this to me? I thought you loved me?" I questioned genuinely.

This felt like a live action nightmare. There he was standing there looking dumbfounded and barely saying anything while my twin used her affair with him to cut me down at the knees. How long had this been going on?

"I do love you. I... baby...I'm sorry. Damn. You haven't been yourself for months. I feel like all you care about is dancing. Getting back to work. We've been engaged for 7 months and you haven't planned anything. We barely even make love anymore. Shit, I barely even see you anymore. I miss you. I miss us..." he said apologetically folding his lips in and pulling me closer to him. "I'm so sorry baby."

Her juices still glistened from his neatly trimmed goatee and her aroma wafted to my nose just as I drew back and slapped him in the face. He flinched and instantly grabbed my wrists preventing me from unleashing anything else.

"Let go of me! You really think I'm gonna stand here talking to you with her pussy on your breath?" I growled struggling against him.

Vanessa watched us with arms folded across her chest and a smirk on her face. "And fuck you too!" I screamed at her.

"Alright, calm down. I'll let you go if-you-calm-down," he spoke slowly to me like I was retarded.

Spit flew from my lips seconds before I launched a knee into his groin the way I learned in self-defense class. I hoped I'd crushed his nuts into a pile of dust as his eyes bulged and he doubled over in pain cupping his genitals. I darted around him wearing a satisfied grin and exited the bedroom barreling barefoot down the stairs, purposely knocking pictures and causing some to fall off the wall.

Grabbing my coat from the piano bench in the foyer, I flung the front door open with a thud and hurried out to my black Land Rover parked in the circular portion of the driveway. Strapped in, I snatched the keys from my coat pocket and cranked it up. My grin widened when I realized Brent's prized silver 2015 Mercedes-Benz CLA45 was parked in front of me.

I reversed a few feet, then accelerated forward ramming the guard bar and more than 2 tons of my truck into the back of it. The thunderous sound of metal colliding rang out as I wrenched forward feeling the bite of the straps against my body. The trunk of the Benz was caved in like a coke can and the back window shattered on impact. The car was pushed a few feet forward before I slammed on the brakes. Thankfully, my airbags didn't deploy. I read somewhere that they usually don't when the collision is under 20 miles per hour anyway.

Collecting myself, I threw the truck in reverse dragging the Benz backwards until the guard bar finally dislodged from the bumper, just as Brent rushed from the house cussing with Vanessa in tow. I threw it back in drive and whipped the steering wheel swiftly around his pile of shit car, then rolled down the passenger's side window to address them.

"You can have this shit too!" I hollered ripping the engagement ring from my finger and hurling it at them. To my delight, it smacked Vanessa right in the face. Laughing hysterically to myself, I screeched off through the outlet recklessly zigzagging over the expensive white Annabelle Hydrangeas and Zelkova flowers aligning both sides of the winding driveway and onto the residential street.

{ 2 }

Yasmin

"Yeah Shawty," he called to me euphorically as my lips descended the length of his shaft once again until his mushroom head nearly touched my tonsils.

It gave me pleasure to return the feeling after the orgasm his tongue just conjured from me minutes before. My pink lady's juices dripped onto my fingers as I flicked and pat my clit and his hands held my head steady to receive his thrusts. Abruptly he released his hold, withdrew himself and sat down on the edge of the bed.

"Bring that pretty ass up here and ride this dick," he ordered lustfully leaning back and holding his rock-hard member.

Doing as I was told, I straddled him without hesitation, licking my lips, locking eyes and lowering my smoldering pussy down onto his stiffness. With every inch I descended, the stresses flooding my mind evaporated into an abyss of moans. His hands gripped my small waist while I rode like a professional jockey trying to win the Triple Crown. Just as I was getting my stride, my phones loud vibrating infiltrated the lulls in our cries as it had been since I arrived, but I didn't break pace. I silently cursed myself for not putting it on silent or turning it off before I got there. Since I was on borrowed time, I was determined to fulfill my sexual cravings before entertaining the drama that probably awaited me.

The climax built between my thighs and I gyrated my hips faster, clenching the walls of my box around him the same way my hands gripped the black dreadlocks that hung thickly on either side of his handsome face. Tugging on them like reins as my body bounced on his bucking hips, my head fell back into oblivion and I cried out, "Yes! Fuck me baby! Oh-my-God-yes!"

"Whose pussy is this?" he questioned ferociously pumping me harder, biting my neck and smacking my ass making me wince.

Through rough pants I leaned forward and snaked my tongue inside of his awaiting mouth. Taking his lower lip between my teeth and cupping his face with fixed eyes I cooed, "Yours!"

Nothing about this man was suitable for a woman in my position except his third leg; but it...was supreme! He palmed my ass firmly with both hands and buried his face into my cleavage as I became dizzy with pleasure and my orgasm engulfed me. Releasing his mane, I crumpled onto his sculpted and tattooed chest as my forbidden fruit released his seeds inside my womb.

Dismounting and laying exhausted beside him with my legs across his thighs, I glimpsed the time on my wristwatch and sighed staring up at the ceiling.

"Damn time flies. I really need to get my ass up out of here. I'm already late," I whined playfully through pants.

My entire morning was spent in court, but I left early to meet up with Dwayne for some well needed release therapy. There always seemed to be enough hours in the day to deal with my heavy case load and family drama but where my needs were concerned...I only had a small window.

He spoke evenly. "It's okay Shawty. It's not like I don't already know what it is. 'Sides, you got me cummin' hard as a muthafucka from this little session right here. If we had any more time to fuck, you'd prolly kill a nigga."

We laughed and a childish grin remained on my face.

"Well, I can't tell. I'm the one over here breathing like Rick Ross jogging a 5K right now. Not you," I teased kissing his muscular arm.

He shifted on his side to face me and palmed the back of my head pulling me in to kiss my forehead. The feel of his soft lips on my skin still gave me butterflies like they had the first time he kissed me.

"I ain't never want no woman like I want you before. Wit' yo' sexy ass," he grinned making me blush. "We so different. But you prolly jus' what I need."

"You make me do things I never thought I'd do before. It's like with you...I can be who I am without worrying about you judging me. I wish we could just run away together and never look back," I told him raising on one elbow and looking him in the eyes.

"Shawty you know we can't do that," he replied placing one finger gently below my chin. "But as for judging you...nah, judging is for people who think they betta' than the next man, ya' feel me? I'own care where a man or woman's at in they life right now...they eat, shit and die just like e'rybody else. Ya' feel me Shawty? But you and me on another level tho'. We got somethin' can't nobody else recreate. You know I ain't no mushy kinda dude. I'own say I love no chicks easy or nothing but...I got love for you Shawty. More than anybody else 'cept for my kids."

I was melting from the inside out with every word and his husky southern street drawl was stirring my juices up again. Just as I was about to respond, my phone's vibration drew both of our attention.

"Yo you popular hard core baby girl. You prolly' wanna answer that fo' as many times as they buzzed that shit."

I huffed getting up and snatched my cell from my bag in the chair by the bed with nothing but attitude. Unlocking the screen, I saw 9 missed calls and 7 text message notifications. Both of my sisters called and left a text message each, but all of the others were from Malik blowing up my phone. I read my sister's messages first.

Tamika: Hey Yas, call me when you get a second. I think Niko left his DS game at your house or in your car and he's driving me nuts looking for it.

Nicky: Why is your husband calling me? You better not have put my name in another one of your lies. You know I can't stand his ass. Call me.

I ran a hand over my face and continued reading my messages.

Malik: Jamilla says you left the office early to meet up with Nicky. Don't forget we have 9:00pm dinner reservations tonight.

Malik: What are you doing? I've called you twice and you're not picking up.

Malik: Okay what the hell are you doing that you can't pick up your phone? Do you have Niko's game in your car? Tamika came by looking for it.

Malik: Why is Nicky's phone sending me straight to voicemail? Where are you?

Malik: I've been texting and calling you for 2 hours now. WTF are you doing? This is unacceptable.

Malik: If we miss these reservations, I'm gonna be pissed off Yasmin. You'd better make it ON TIME.

"Shit," I shrieked dropping my phone down on the chair and beginning to scramble for my things.

I slipped into my bra and gray skirt in record time under Dwayne's watchful eyes and swiped my shirt off the floor by the bed.

"What's wrong?" he asked with an amused raised brow. "Yo' you movin' fast as fuck Shawty. Is somethin' on fire?"

"May as well be. I let the time slip away from me and now I'm late. Tamika called Malik looking for Niko's game and he called Nicky because I'm supposed to be with her. Now I gotta explain to everybody where I've been and get home in time for dinner reservations at 9."

"I'on think you gon' make it Shawty," he said nonchalantly leaning back on the pillows as I spotted one gray pump nearby and slid my foot into it before hobbling over to put on the other.

"I'm about to try though," I told him grabbing my bag and dashing into the bathroom.

I swear this pixie cut was a lifesaver. I finger combed through my hair and smoothed down some sweat curled edges with a brush in the mirror. Most of my lipstick was gone but the light makeup I applied this morning was otherwise still flawless over my milk chocolate skin. I swished some mouthwash around in my mouth, spit and used a soaped-up face cloth to wipe my face and take a bird bath. Reapplying MAC's Cremesheen pink lipstick, I finished off my look and tossed everything but the cloth back into my bag.

Hastily buttoning my teal shirt from the bottom, I stepped back from the mirror inspecting my slender figure and smoothing out the wrinkles. My cousin Amina always said I looked like Melinda Williams, Bird on the TV show Soul Food. Most people agreed and I liked the comparison, so I got my hair cut in her signature style.

Dwayne was hovering over the table near the sliding balcony doors with his back to me when I reentered the room. Umm umm umm. I admired his 6'0" muscular physique and the way each tattoo accentuated the pecan tone of his sculpted body. He favored the rapper Waka Flocka Flame in a lot of ways from his height, dreadlocks and tattoos down to the gold he frequently wore in his mouth. Rounding him, I saw the ingredients for the blunt laid on the table as his hanging dreads obscured his face.

"You know this is a non-smoking room baby," I teasingly chastised already knowing it wouldn't deter him from doing what he planned.

He smiled wide exposing the shiny gold and diamond filled grill covering the top row of his teeth and licked his lips seductively.

"It's only one Shawty. You know ya' boy gotta blaze one after you put that pow yow on me. I'll go out there," he said nodding towards the balcony.

"Uh uh," I shook my head sideways and embraced him around the waist massaging his sleeping dragon. "What if somebody smells it and calls security?"

He looked down at me thoughtfully, still grinning. "That's why we need to stop comin' to these ol' fuck nigga bougie hotels then. All we really need is a sturdy bed anyway. And if you keep playin' wit' my lil' man like that...I'm gone fuck you back outta yo' clothes again and you're not gonna be going nowhere Shawty."

I smiled devilishly inhaling the scent of his Sean John 3 AM cologne and kissing him on the neck. "We are in a nooo smoking room Dwayne. That means nooo smoking."

He huffed, returned my embrace with his hands extending to my ass and bowed his head to make the tips of our noses touch. "Alright Miss Yasmin. But next time I'm pickin' the place. I'm 'bout to shower and head out right behind you then. Did you leave me that?"

I nodded and kissed him deeply before separating. He slapped me on the ass playfully and I yelped laughing while strutting to retrieve my bag and phone.

"I'll call you," I threw over my shoulder leaving the hotel room.

Standing at the elevator my fingers scrolled to Tamika's number just as it vibrated in my hand and Malik's face flashed on my screen. I exhaled and forced pleasantry into my voice amidst my frown.

"Hey honey."

"Hey yourself. Where are you?" He started in immediately.

It was nearly a quarter to 9 so he was definitely about to be on 10 about the reservations.

"Leaving the mall. I'm sorry bae. I forgot to turn my ringer back on when I left court this afternoon and I just noticed it like 10 minutes ago."

"Really? I thought you were supposed to be out with Nicky? What happened to that? Because neither of y'all are bothering to pick up your damn phones."

I coughed loudly trying to mask the elevator ding as the doors opened and I pulled the diamond nooses from my bag slipping them on my ring finger.

"Yeah, I was out with her but then she let me for a date, and I decided to stay out shopping. I haven't had a chance to do it in a long time believe it or not and I ended up running into one of my sorors I haven't seen since graduation. I must've lost track of time. I don't know why Nicky's not picking up her phone; but like I said, I didn't realize my phone was on silent still," I lied.

"All day though? And you didn't think to check your phone the entire time? How did you even link up with Nicky if your phone was off? Which mall are you in anyway?" he asked curtly.

"We already had a set spot to meet so I didn't need my phone on to go shopping with her Columbo. We went to a few malls but I'm just now leaving Lenox Mall. Stop grilling me like a child Malik. I was excited to see my girl and I never even thought to look at my phone. I literally had my finger on the button about to call you when it rang in my hand just now."

There was a long pause which usually meant he was considering the validity of my story. I was soooo not in the mood for his adult parenting.

"So, you left Nicky and went to hang with who?"

"Nicky left me to go on a date I told you. Anika. My line sister. What do you need? DNA?" I retorted rattling off a random soror's name.

"And as much as you post on Facebook you didn't post a picture with her? That doesn't even make sense to me Yasmine."

"Malik, I'm starting not to give a damn what makes sense to you. She works for the FBI and is very private so I already knew she wouldn't take a picture. She doesn't even have a Facebook account at all. I can't be out with a friend without taking a picture now?" I argued trying to stump him.

"So you complain that we don't do anything together except work. I plan a nice dinner for us; tell you in advance; and you don't show up. This is what I mean when I say you don't respect my time," he said switching subjects.

"I do respect your time Malik. It was an innocent mistake. I was enjoying time with my friend and lost track of time. Am I not allowed to make mistakes? I'm sorry I'm not as perfect as you are. I'm on my way home now so we can still go if you just call and change the time to 9:30 or 10:00. I'm only a half hour away."

He blew out an irritated breath.

"Just like that, huh? You blow off what I have planned, and everything is supposed to be okay with a reschedule? No apology. No—"

"What do you mean 'no apology'? I said I was sorry. What the hell else can I do? The time is already gone Malik," I interrupted his rant as I leisurely approached my car in the dimly lit Sheraton's parking deck. They were doing repairs on the entire hotel and it's parking areas so their patronage wasn't as high as usual and I knew the likelihood of me running into a familiar face would be less here.

"I am on my way now. Why do you have to make everything a big deal?"

A cool breeze whisked up my skirt and I bit my bottom lip thinking of the way Dwayne teased and blew on those same throbbing lips earlier. I definitely felt naughty going out in public with no panties on. Dwayne made sure I left them with him after every encounter. I really have no idea what he did with them but I assumed it was something freaky and that kind of turned me on too. It has been eons since Malik made me feel as giddy as Dwayne has. In fact, I hadn't even felt his lips on my lower ones for more than a few rushed minutes at a time in years. Yet here I was...headed back to purgatory anyway.

"Oh, am I making too much out of it? Excuse me for being upset because I changed my schedule around to spend some quality time with my wife who didn't bother to answer my calls or texts for hours. It's these types of careless indiscretions that give me pause about us having kids Yasmin. You're still too selfish to play mother. You haven't changed one bit from when we were in college and I'm certainly not going to give up my career to—"

"What? I know you didn't just call me selfish when you're the one who's always too busy for me even when you're standing right in my face or to even go to marriage counseling!" I yelled losing my entire cool on this motherfucker. "My nephews aren't always begging to stay the night at Auntie Yas's house because I'm selfish and bad with kids Malik. I take exception to your insult because I make time when it's important. What do you make time for? Or should I say who do you make time for?" I hissed.

Silence befell the other end except for his heavy breathing.

"Yasmin, you know...listen..." he rushed then paused before clearing his throat. "There is no who for you to worry about. And I said that I would go to counseling; we just need to find the right one for us. Look baby; why don't you just come on home. I'll call Aqua Blue and see if I can move the reservation, and we can talk about this calmly face to face over a nice dinner."

"Malik, I'm getting off the phone now. I don't have my bluetooth charged and I can't hold the phone while I'm driving. I'll see you in a half hour," I said dryly unlocking the doors to my white Lexus with the keyfob in hand.

We'd had a million face to face conversations about our failing marriage before and frankly, without counseling, there wasn't much more to say that wouldn't result in an argument.

"Alright baby. Get home safely."

Baby. I mocked in my mind hanging up with a concurrent eye roll slipping my phone in a side pocket. I wished I could get in and drive in the opposite direction of my nagging ball and chain, but such was my life. I opened my car door and was shoved abruptly from the back against the open frame once it was ajar. Before I could react, I felt the barrel of a gun against my temple.

"Give me your purse and your keys!" a raspy voice ordered.

"Oh my God. You can have every—"

"Shut up!" he yelled yanking me backwards and turning me around to face him.

He was about 5'10" or 11" wearing all black with a black Raiders cap pulled down over his eyes and a red bandana covering his face as he snatched my bag with the hammer held steady in my face. Tears streaked my cheeks and my bladder threatened to release its own stream as he continued yelling.

"Keys! Keys! Give me the fucking keys!" he barked darting his eyes around the lot and then back to me.

I hurriedly gave them up and silently prayed God this man wouldn't leave my panty-less body in this hotel parking lot where I'm not supposed to be. I trembled at the thought of what might be about to happen to me while his narrowed beady eyes sized me up.

"The rings too," he said through clenched teeth before hitting me in the head with the butt of the gun.

I cried out in pain crumpling to the ground and grabbing my wound.

"Please..." I begged.

"Hurry the fuck up!" he spat.

My hands shook as I wrenched the rings from my finger and handed them to him staring up at his masked face. He was familiar to me somehow. His cologne. His glaring eyes. Still, I was just happy he hadn't seen fit to blow my brains onto the pavement yet.

"You know me?" he questioned me kneeling down with the gun in my face again as I shook my head no vigorously. "Why the fuck you keep looking at me then?"

"I... I'm sorry," I said meekly cringing as trickles of urine leaked down my leg.

There was dead silence as he glared disgustedly at the soiled asphalt and then to me.

"Get up," he demanded menacingly while I struggled to my feet.

Once standing, he shoved me roughly away from the car causing me to fall again and aimed his gun at me. I squeezed my eyes shut and braced myself for the bullets I knew he was about to let off into my trembling body. Instead, I heard a car door slam and the wheels screech off as he burned rubber from the lot.

{ 3 }

Amina

I smiled politely handing the valet a 10 spot before he ushered me into the driver's seat of my convertible cherry red Jaguar eyeing my ass as he shut the door. I checked my makeup, primped my slick back ponytail in the rear-view mirror and threw my car in drive cranking up the volume on Jazmine Sullivan's song "Mascara".

So, I never leave the hooouse...withooout... make-up ooon,
I keep mascara in my pocket if I'm running to the market
'Cause you never know...who's...wa-tching you
So I got to stay on, I got to stay on
I got to stay ooon, I got to stay on
Said I got to stay ooon!

It was almost 10 o'clock but it was the first time in a loooong time that I'd had a date or was headed home from one before midnight. I was beaming because it was my last one and was not only lucrative, but easy. I sang along happily with Jazmine as though I was performing on stage until I was interrupted at a red light by some crusty lipped black dude with tats on his face and matted dreads in a neon green Impala.

"Ay Ms. Lady! Ay! Ay! Where you headed?" he yelled over the sound of an unknown rap song blasting from his speakers.

I cocked an amused eyebrow at him without response as I pulled my Chanel sunglasses from the visor and placed them on my face.

Evening shade. Ol' boy really needed to stop smoking whatever it was that made him think he was even close to being on my level. The fool then turned down his radio and continued soliciting me as though the loud music was the reason why he was being ignored.

"Where you headed sexy lady? You should let me get your number," he shouted licking his cracked mouthpiece.

He reminded me of that guy Puma on Black Ink causing me to smirk though my stomach churned at the mere thought of anyone from that cast touching me. Yeesh! My foot hit the gas the second the light turned green and I sped down West Peachtree like a bat out of hell away from his dusty ass feeling itchy. Don't get me wrong, I don't fault him for wanting to approach me. In fact, it would've been more unusual if he hadn't. But c'mon now. Dudes need to know the difference between desirable and attainable. I'm a confident, mocha-toned, 5'9" bomb shell with hazel-eyes and naturally long healthy hair that flows down my back. Judging by the few pageants I've won, modeling gigs I've landed and the jaws most men have to pick up as I pass them on a daily basis, I'm a beautiful woman by anyone's standards even at 29. Therefore, I don't think it's being vein when I tell you I'm a certified dime piece. I'm simply being honest.

My android chimed inside my Tory Burch bag and automatically switched to ringing through the car connection which instantly paused the music. The number on the screen in my dashboard wasn't linked to a name in my phone but I answered anyway from the phone option on my steering wheel.

"Hello."

"Hey beautiful, this is Donovan. How are you?"

I squinted in thought for a few seconds before I remembered he was the sexy tall, dark and fine Lance Gross double I met the week before. The morning I closed on my house, I had to do a final walk through with the builder and my agent to notate any issues that may still need fixing since it was a new build. When my agent Cassandra introduced the 6'3" chocolate man wearing gray sweatpants, work boots and a gray ribbed tank top with paint splotches on it as the builder, the space between my legs got a little moist. He was probably in his late 20's or early 30's with a slim but muscular build and piercing brown eyes which were glued to every curve displayed in the black fitted Donna Karan jumper I wore.

I rarely entertained the thought of dating any man I hadn't met via my typical dating practices, but there was something about this guy that made my heart palpitate faster than most. Admittedly, it was probably the bulge in his pants despite the culprit being flaccid and the way his pearly whites complimented his dark complexion. Unlike most single women my age though, I wasn't looking for a boyfriend, husband or children to stress my life, so a fling of the flesh with him would certainly be doable. In my profession, I'd come across enough men leading double lives to completely turn me off to the idea of commitment for eternity. Amina Douglas is only focused on 3 things. My money, my family and myself.

I was actually a little impressed that he'd taken this long to call me considering his inability to take his eyes off of me when we met.

"I'm fine, and yourself?" I replied.

"Better now that I'm talking to you," he said in a deep voice.

"Oh my God. Are you really this cheesy?" I chuckled leaning an elbow on the door.

I truly hoped he wasn't going to turn out to be one of those dudes who thinks every word out of his mouth is Idris Elba sexy. If so, this was going to be a short conversation because I wasn't in the mood.

"Ahhhh that hurts. Cheesy? I thought I was being charming," he retorted laughing.

"Oh, is that what that was? Because it sounded like some ol' Billy Dee Williams 101 starter line to me."

"Damn, so you're just gonna start right off hurting a brotha's feelings huh?" he asked playfully.

"Only if it's that easy."

"No. Actually, it's not. I like a woman with a good sense of humor. So, did I catch you at a bad time? You sound like you're out an about."

"I am. But I can talk if you can."

At least he wasn't a pussy. In my experience, some of the finest of men usually had the most fragile egos because they expected women to fawn over them like schoolgirls and when a woman didn't, they felt emasculated. Cue Ralph Tresvant's song "Sensitivity" for those wussies. Ha ha!

"Are you headed out or headed in?" he asked.

"I'm sorry what?"

"I said are you on your way out or on your way home?"

"Oh. Headed home," I told him pushing the button to close the drop top.

The April wind blowing through my car was already starting to make the conversation choppy and I knew it would only get worse once I hit the highway.

"I figured I'd let you settle in your new place before I started to blowing up your phone," he joked. "I was surprised when you said it was just going to be you in that big house. I believe all of the other 4-bedroom floor plans were bought by families. That's a lot of space for one person unless you're a celebrity or something? Come to think of it, you do kind of favor Kenya Moore. Any relation?"

I giggled. This wasn't the first time I've been compared to that bat-shit crazy chick from Housewives of Atlanta though. Before she got on the show, I was proud of the comparison to the former Miss U.S.A. After all, she is beautiful. But now that she's more popular for her ratchet TV moments...umm...not so much.

"Uh...No. And how do you know I don't have kids?" I questioned.

"Oh, my bad. How many kids do you have?"

"I don't have any kids. I was just saying that you assumed I didn't without knowing."

He chuckled again. "Okay okay. You're right. So, what are your plans for the extra 3 rooms since you don't have any kids? Do you entertain a lot?"

"One room is going to be converted into a closet and dressing room, one is gonna be my studio and the other will be a spare bedroom for guests. I wouldn't say I entertain a lot. But I am pretty tight with my family."

"Oh, okay that's cool. So, a studio huh? What do you do, sing?"

"No. An art studio. I draw and paint mostly."

"Really? I do a little sculpting myself. I've always been good with my hands," he said as dirty thoughts ran through my head at what other things his hands might be good at. "So, is that what you do for a living? Are you an artist?"

"Not at all. I'm a decoy for a private investigation agency. Something like bait for cheaters in most cases," I uttered the stock answer I always gave.

"Like some Charlie's Angel's kinda thing where you go undercover? Ha! You are full of surprises," he teased.

"Well, it's not quite like that," I laughed seeing another call coming through. "Hey, can you hold on for a minute? I have another call on the line."

He agreed and I clicked over just as I was approaching my exit.

"Hey Val, I got another call on the line. Lemme' call you right back when I get off," I said as soon as I switched over already knowing from the caller ID who it was.

"Oh...okay. Yeah, call me back," she said sobbing.

Aww hell. The last time she called like this she'd just been told her Achilles tendon injury was gonna need surgery and she was gonna be out of work for 6 months.

"Wait. What's wrong?" I asked concerned.

"Everything. Everything is wrong," she cried.

"Okay. Hold on, let me get rid of this call and we can talk," I told her as soon as she said that and instantly switched back to Donovan.

"Hey...Donovan this is my cousin and she's going through something so I really need to take this. Can I call you back?"

"Sure, I understand. I hope she's okay. I'll talk to you later then," he said politely.

"Thank you. Good night," I told him quickly and clicked back.

Of all of my cousins, I'm the closest to Valerie, which is surprising because she's probably the most conservative and least fashion forward relative I have. Still, she's not the overly dramatic type at all, so if she was calling me bent out of shape, I was automatically bent out of shape too because it had to be something serious. I just hoped it didn't have anything else to do with her injury because she'd been working really hard in physical therapy to get herself back in condition to perform again. We all have passions, but dancing is more than a passion for Val. From the time she started dancing as a kid, it was easy to see the girl lived and breathed it. I think it's probably the only thing she's ever really cared about besides family and her fiancé. Humph...probably in that order too.

"Alright Val. What happened?" I asked softly.

"He...he's cheating on me with Vanessa," she blubbered causing my eyes to bug out of my head as I pulled into my driveway activating the garage door.

I knew what it sounded like she said, but I had to have heard her wrong 'cause I know damn good and well that wasn't right.

"Umm...what?" I questioned hoping she was simply too distraught to have compiled her words correctly the first time.

"Brent! The asshole has been fucking my sister behind my back!" she screamed so angrily I could almost hear the spit flying from her mouth.

I drove in, parked and fell back into my seat with my mouth agape staring blankly at the wall through my windshield. Vanessa had to be out of her rabbit assed mind to do some shit like this. I hated to say it though, Brent's behavior wasn't that surprising. I never liked his arrogant and controlling ass in the first place for Valerie, but it wasn't my place to throw salt in her relationship.

"Holy shit. How do you know that?" Is all I could eke out.

This was too bananas for my mind to even grasp! Vanessa has always been a grimy bitch, but this had to be an all-time low for her? Val continued to talk as I switched the feed from my car back to my cell and turned the ignition off.

"I know because I saw it for myself! I went over to surprise him and I'm the one who got surprised to see his tongue in her pussy," she sobbed harder. "I don't...even know...how long they've been fucking. But this...wasn't...the first time," she spoke between cries.

I was shaking my head in disgust and grabbing my bag from the passenger's seat. Placing it on one shoulder as I exited the car, I put my sunglasses on top of my head and placed the phone to my ear.

"Brent is a piece a shit with his old Milk Dud head having ass. All these men out here and she's gotta get with her twin sister's fiancé? I mean where they do that at? I hope you beat Vanessa's ass into a coma too because if you didn't, I'm gonna do it when I see her low-down ass."

"We fought. You know I'm not really a fighter, but I caught her a few good times and I tried to impale both of them with the heel of my shoe. At the end of the day, I just ended up kneeing that bastard in the balls, knocking shit off the walls in his house and crashing up his Benz."

"Crashing up his Benz?" I bellowed excitedly walking outside my garage and down the driveway to the mailbox just as a black Ford Explorer drove slowly past on the street. "That's the new car he just got right? Ha ha ha! Good for his ass then!"

She forced a giggle through tears and said, "Well I was mad as hell and since I couldn't really beat either of their asses, I went to fucking up his property. I got in my Land Rover and rammed his precious new car into a sardine can and then I drove all over his expensive flowers on my way out."

"Awww hell! That's what I'm talking about!" We were both laughing then except hers were through sniffles. "Oh yeah I'm sure that hurt just as bad if not worse than you crushing his nuts."

"And I threw his ring out the window and smacked that bitch right in the face with it too," she continued more animatedly.

I paused and gave a side eye to the cell that she couldn't see as I approached my mailbox and pulled the pile of envelopes from it.

"Umm...that ring was what...3 or 4 carats? Shiiiit...he would've had to pry that ring off of my cold dead hand to get it back after what he did. Or I'd have pawned the bitch," I said rolling my eyes and placing the phone between my ear and shoulder while I walked sorting through my mail.

"I wasn't even thinking about all of that. I was just so angry I didn't want any parts of him. I mean we've been together for almost 2 years. I moved back to Atlanta for him. I could've just stayed my black ass in New York if he didn't want to be with me anymore. So, what if I hadn't started planning the wedding yet. I was in the middle of recovering from a torn Achilles tendon. It wasn't like I had a sprained ankle Amina. I mean it could've ended my entire dance career. Hell, it still can! And here the both of these motherfuckers were keke-ing all up in my face for only God knows how long while they were screwing behind my back. I feel so dirty!"

I could hear the pain in her voice and only imagine the anger, hurt and humiliation she must've felt seeing it live and in person. She didn't deserve this from him or from Vanessa.

"I know you're hurting right now but at least you found out before you actually ended up married to his ass. So what are you gonna do now? Because I know you're not still gonna move in with that bastard now."

"Hell no!" she exclaimed. "But he really stuck me now though. My lease is up next week because I was supposed to be moving in with him then. Eighty-five percent of everything is packed already and my money is messed up since I've been out of work for so long. He's been paying all of my bills and covering my medical copays and stuff since I hurt myself. I have just over two grand to my name right now."

"If you don't count how much you can get for the ring," I told her with a laugh.

"True."

"Well, you can always come stay with me until..."

Pow! Pow! Pow!

The familiar explosive sounds rang out as I jolted forward dropping everything and falling to my hands and knees. The world seemed to slow down at the same time my heart raced, and the air got thinner as my breathing became labored. My back and side burned like someone was branding me and my vision was blurring from the onslaught of tears welling in my eyes. I placed one hand on my side where it felt like a hot poker was sticking me and felt a warm, wet and sticky liquid. I already knew what I would find but the confirmation made me panic even more. I didn't want to die. I didn't deserve to die either.

"Help," I murmured viewing my red palm as tears dropped onto the concrete and the sound of Valerie hysterically screaming my name began to register.

My mind was everywhere and nowhere at the same time. I tried to crawl towards the garage, but my limbs felt like rubber as I silently prayed the gunman wouldn't come up behind me and deliver a kill shot.

"Help...me," I struggled to voice again before the driveway suddenly rose up and slammed into my face.

{ 4 }

Vanessa

I sat on the chaise in front of the picture window overlooking Brent's manicured lawn and blew smoke rings through one of the open panes toward the moonlight. There was definitely going to be a shit storm headed my way as soon as my sister whined to everybody in my family. I was already only one step below Tamika on the black sheep of the family list and that's only because she has 3 babies by 3 baby daddies and a G.E.D. Whatever though. None of them pay my bills.

"Put that out," Brent snapped entering the bedroom from the master bath wearing nothing but black Givenchy sweatpants and a scowl on his face.

He was definitely a sexy man...until he opened his controlling mouth. I rolled my eyes and took one last drag of my cigarette before dashing it out on the outside of the sill.

"Calm down," I told him flicking it out the window.

"What the hell is wrong with you?" he asked incredulously craning his neck chasing the demise of my cigarette with his eyes.

I crossed my arms and huffed. He was lucky I flicked it out of the window and not at him after the way he'd been talking to me since the Flying Nun departed tearing up his shit. He'd been getting high and raging around the house bitching at me for telling her too much even while I was helping him tend to his injuries. It wasn't my fault she was too dense and caught up in herself to realize when her man was slipping, and I really didn't owe either of them any loyalties.

"Respect my shit. I keep telling you not to smoke in my house. It's a nasty habit and tossing your cigarette out on my lawn is just disrespectful. I should make you go pick it up from out there and throw it in the garbage where it belongs," he scolded.

I chuckled. "Make me go pick it up? Negro please. You can't make me do a damn thing. You have lawn care people anyway, don't you? I'm sure one of them will get it. It's not like it was lit. I don't know what you have an attitude with me for anyway. I'm not the one who smashed your car."

His face tightened as he winced and touched the gauze pad secured against the wound between his neck and shoulder with medical tape. Most of the scratches and gashes she inflicted were minor on his back but that one was pretty deep. We cleaned them all with alcohol and covered some with Band-Aids. Brother was not only a germaphobe, but his master bathroom closet was stocked like a pharmacy for most illnesses or injuries. He had every size and fabric of Band-Aid you could shop for, medical tape, gauze, splints, a ton of antiseptics, sanitizers and ointments, various thermometers, surgical masks, medications for colds, headaches, back pain, allergies, diarrhea, constipation, insomnia and a slew of other stuff.

No wonder Dr. Quinn Medicine Man didn't mind hosting Valerie over here for months after her surgery. Besides having a housekeeper on staff 4 days a week, he was more than prepared for his house to double as a sick bay. Although I'd been here a number of times both visiting my sister and alone, I hadn't ever snooped around in his master bathroom.

"Shut up Vanessa," he scoffed pulling a white baggy from his nightstand and walking it over to the glass coffee table in the sitting room area of his bedroom.

"You shut up," I shot back frowning. "You're gonna OD on that shit. It's a nasty habit," I mocked.

He waved me off and proceeded. Here his salty ass was complaining about a little harmless cigarette smoke, but he was 'bout to put another round of coke up his nose. He was way looser around me than he was around Valerie. That moron has no idea that he messes with that white girl and she's supposed to be his fiancée. Now I'm no angel, but the hardest drug I'll do is weed. Everything else is expensive and takes its toll on your body sooner or later if it doesn't get your mind first. That, and his bullshit attitude was my cue to leave. The tow truck took his car to a repair shop in Buckhead earlier and though he had 2 other cars garaged on the property, he was still 38-hot about her smashing his new pride and joy and taking it out on me.

He'd scooped me from my house so I didn't have my own car but Uber would do. I slid my feet into the black Gucci sandals I scavenged from Valerie's closet last week and tightened the ankle straps while he sniffed thin white lines from the table top with a rolled up bill. Grabbing my purse and phone from the top of his dresser I swiped the screen to my Uber app and proceeded to enter my location information as I headed toward the door without a word.

I know y'all think I'm grimy for sleeping with my sister's fiancé but believe me when I tell you she was simply wasting the man. She's a basic chick with basic needs so locking down a man like Brent who likes to spoil his woman with extravagant gifts, trips or whatever their heart desires was wasteful. She's never cared about designer clothes, expensive jewelry, big cars or big houses like normal women. She's...basic. She even mentioned to me once that she thought Brent having this huge 6-bedroom mansion was a waste of money and space for a single man. Valerie was a small fish in a big pond, and it was a no-brainer that I'm the better catch. Period.

"Hold up. Hold up. Where you going? You leaving?" he asked wiping residue from his nose and sitting back on the couch with his eyes already glazed from his earlier taste.

"Of course. You're acting like an ass and I have other things to do anyway. Can I get some money for Uber?" I huffed.

"Things like what? I thought I was your something to do tonight," he said grinning.

I rolled my eyes. "Yeah, well this isn't what it was supposed to be so I'm about to be out."

"Look, I'm sorry for snapping off on you but...you know I'm just pissed off at everything. I'm all cut up; she blew through my house like a tornado and crashed my car...that ripped Joseph Scorselo painting is worth almost 25 grand you know?" he told me with furrowed brows. "My shit is expensive. And you taunting her was just making it worse. Regardless of what we've been doing here, you knew I didn't want Valerie to know about us. We're not permanent. She is. That girl is my heart."

I laughed sarcastically. "Yeah, well your heart must not have communicated that with your dick. It's not like I planned for her to walk in on us but it is what it is. You're just as guilty as I am so I'm not gonna stand around while you pop off at the mouth at me because we got caught. You could've stopped at any time Boo. But you kept calling so...let's not forget that this wasn't the first time. I'm not the one who's engaged while you're bitchin'. You had needs; I had needs; and we satisfied them. I certainly didn't force you to cheat. You could've been upstanding and just broke up with her, but you didn't."

He ran his hand over his face and spread his arms across the back of the couch.

"I never wanted to break up with her at all. But we're not married yet so I'm just getting some things out of my system before we are. I just gotta talk to her and explain. We love each other. She'll forgive me," he said spastically.

I twisted my lips with one hand on my hip. "How high are you? Because you must be baked if you think she's gonna forgive you. Even if she would, once she blabs all of this to our family, they're definitely gonna want your head on a platter. Especially my brother, who'll probably end up on your doorstep ready to kick your ass. What exactly is it about her that you love so much anyway? She's had months of downtime and hasn't planned anything for your wedding. You buy her all those expensive gifts and clothes and all that shit just sits in her closet gathering dust unless I snag it because she never wants to go anywhere. And why would you want to marry a woman who doesn't satisfy you sexually anyway? Hell, I'm bored just recapping what the bitch doesn't do. So, enlighten me. What is it that you love soooo much about her?"

Brent rubbed his chin and stared at me with glazed eyes like he was mulling over what to say...or maybe he was just super high. I don't know.

"Vanessa knock it off. Stop trying to pick my brain. I never said she doesn't satisfy me in bed either."

"Oh, you didn't? So, you didn't say I gave you the best head you've ever had? You don't lust for me like a vampire after I let you taste and feel this pussy?" I smirked.

He cut his eyes at me. "How much you need for Uber?"

I chuckled. So now he was ready for me to go. My feelings weren't hurt though because I had none invested in him at all. He was simply a toy that I enjoyed playing with since he couldn't keep his eyes off of me whenever I was around, and I knew Val wasn't holding him down right. He took every opportunity possible to ogle me and make small talk before and after I visited Val at his place. He had more compliments than my Instagram followers and the opportunity to get some extra paper from a man like him who loves tossing it around anyway wasn't lost on me.

He and his brother Dean are heirs to the Lincoln Hotel chain fortune, so they've got money to burn. Both of them have figure head job titles at the hotel in Atlanta with high paying salaries but really don't do shit to deserve them from what I know. Dudes born with silver spoons in their mouths don't know what it's like not to get what they want, and I'm okay with that as long as I get what I want when what they want is me.

If he'd met me instead of Val's barefaced, off-name brand shopping ass when she performed at the MET in New York, she wouldn't have even been on his radar. The Lincoln's are originally from New York and that is where the original Hotel was built so expectedly, Brent travels to the state frequently. They dated for almost a year long distance before she decided to move back to Atlanta and dance for the Alvin Ailey company here. Somehow, little miss perfect always ends up coming out on top regardless of whether she deserves to or not. Her recent injury is probably the first instance of defeat or heartache she's ever had to suffer; before catching me with her man that is. My family decided when we were in junior high that she was something special and obviously everyone else, including her, agreed.

In the third grade, my mom put us both in ballet with my cousins Amina and Yasmin because we were all the same age and were practically inseparable as kids. Me and Yasmin hated it and convinced my mom to let us quit by the fourth grade, but Valerie and Amina took to the classes like swans. By our last year in junior high Amina had lost interest in everything but boys and Valerie convinced my mom to enroll her in some kind of African Jazz classes instead. Well one of the instructors there recommended she take advanced classes since she was so good and the next thing I knew, my mom was on the phone with my Uncle Derrick who taught at the school FAME was based on in New York, raving about Val like she was Debbie Allen or somebody.

Uncle Derrick set up an audition and what do you know, the golden child aced it. I was happy for her, but I couldn't believe my parents were actually letting her move to New York to live with my uncle and his live-in girlfriend for the entire 4 years. How do you agree to separate your kids like that? Especially when we're identical twins who've never been apart for more than 24 hours. Even more offensive and insensitive was the fact that my own sister could be so selfish and leave me behind without a second thought. We used to finish each other's sentences and would sit for hours in our room together just enjoying each other's company. We hated dressing alike because people constantly compared us to those ugly Tia and Tamara Mowry twins, but we kept it similar and did almost everything together. There were other performing arts schools in Atlanta she could've attended but they never even looked at that because my uncle worked for La-Guardia.

In high school, every time I turned around after that it was Valerie this or Valerie that, meanwhile my parents rode my ass like a tractor if I even breathed wrong. Still, high school is where I came into my own because her absence gave me the strength to be myself 100% instead of mirroring some of Valerie's actions or caring what she thought. I started being selfish too. If it was okay for her, then it was okay for me. And one thing I was not going to do was allow myself to depend on any of my cousins or anybody else to validate or support me again. If the bitch I shared identical DNA with could turn her back on me and barely even call to see how I was doing, then somebody else would damn sure do it.

Freshman year my breasts and apple bottom started poking out too, so you know the boys were on me like white on rice. Me and a hot little Latin transplant from the Dominican Republic named Delia became fast friends as the obvious two baddest bitches in the ninth grade. She's the one who put me up on the latest fashion labels and showed me how to apply my make up with skill. Before anybody knew it, I was not only turning the heads of my classmates, but my teachers too.

Unlike Valerie who was always doing the most in and outside of school to impress my parents, I did the bare minimum to ensure I got passing grades because I planned to be a famous singer like Janet Jackson and Beyoncé. Valerie wasn't the only talented twin; but when I wanted them to pay for singing lessons for me to hone my talent, my dad said they cost too much. When I stood in line hours for American Idol auditions, nobody but my cousin Tamika and my girls Delia and Rachel bothered to come down there with me. Even though I never made it through to the judge's round, I bet if it had been Valerie auditioning for So You Think You Can Dance, every Vincent, Graham and Douglas would have been front and center.

We both graduated on time but once Val got into Julliard...forget about it. She might as well have walked on water to travel back and forth to Atlanta for visits the way everybody praised her. But even though I got into the California College of Music, my parents acted like they were too strapped to pay for it all. Yeah, I could've gotten student loans myself but why should I have had to when Valerie didn't? They weren't paying all of her schooling either, but Val had my Uncle Derrick helping her out too...like she was his daughter. Shit, I'd probably be at least Rihanna by now if my family had rallied for me even half as much as they had for Twinkle toes. Valerie was spoon fed her success while I was out here grinding to get mine with or without my family behind me.

"Alright well where's the money so I can go?" I asked smartly.

He went to the top draw of his nightstand and handed me a wad of cash.

"Here. And don't say anything else to Val," he ordered going back to his couch and flipping on the mounted flat screen with the remote off the end table.

I gas faced him and debated on whether or not to check his black ass for trying to dictate who I could and couldn't talk to, but decided against it. There was no reason for me to waste my breath on him in his current state, but I would read him his rights the next time he picked up his phone to call me. And believe me...he would.

I thumbed through the money as I descended the stairs to the first floor and counted out 300 dollars. Obviously, the Uber wasn't going to cost that much but either he was too high to notice or too guilty to care. Ten minutes later I was in the backseat of a green Ford Focus headed to my place across town. I got a call from my mother, but I sent it to voicemail just in case the crybaby had already started telling. When I arrived, I didn't waste any time going inside and changing into black leggings, a black long sleeve shirt and black Air Force One's. It was late enough now that the buses were ending their run and the foot traffic where I was headed would have died down so that I could easily execute my plan unseen. I put on the black Cleopatra wig I'd worn for Halloween, grabbed my gloves and rocked my black matte Emporio Armani sunglasses as I got into my black Beamer and cranked her up. Within 15-minutes I was a quarter mile away from my destination where I parked in a nearby Kroger and trekked it through the lot.

There was a large grassy lot that had yet to be developed spanning a few acres across the back of a row of houses directly in my line of sight. Once I crept through the lot, I retrieved the red plastic canister I'd stashed from the shrubs beside the backdoor of a specific medium sized 2 story home and scanned my surroundings for onlookers. I didn't see anyone and didn't think I would since it was a predominantly quiet neighborhood. I quickly doused the circumference of the house with the contents of the container and glanced up at the light shining from a back-bedroom window. I smiled wickedly, glad the occupant was right where I wanted them to be as I began drenching the panels directly under the window before emptying the rest on the backdoor, porch and shrubs.

The thick smell of gasoline was becoming nauseating, so I pulled a sleeve up to cover my nose from the smell and tried to mouth breathe as much as possible. Pulling the barbecue lighter from my waist with one gloved hand and tossing the canister on top of the shrubs with the other, I leaned down and lit the damp area directly in front of me. Not taking the time to watch as the fire ate its way around the property, I walked briskly through the tall grass until I reached the outlet and then walked leisurely back to the Kroger lot. Dark clouds of smoke rose into the sky signaling my handy work in the distance as I drove off in the opposite direction pulling a Newport from a pack in the cup holder and lighting it.

{ 5 }

Valerie

Brent: Baby, please give me a chance to explain myself. I love you. Let's not throw away everything for one mistake. Can I come talk to you face to face?

Me: Fuck You. Talk about what? You should've been talking to me before you started fucking my sister. If I see your face, I just might smash it in!

Brent: I should have. But we were having problems Val. I'm not blaming you but you know we haven't been right. I'm sorry.

Me: You are sorry! Leave me alone!

Brent: I can't baby. I want to make this right. I don't want her. I want you. I've just been going through something.

Me: You've been going through my sister! How long have you been doing it Brent? Is that bitch with you right now? Because she's sure as hell not here with us and I know my mother called her.

Brent: Here where? I sent her home. We're not together. I don't love her. I love YOU. Can we please talk? Answer your phone baby.

If not for the fact that my tear ducts were probably all dried up from crying over his sorry ass, and then over Amina being shot, I might have been able to dredge up an angry one to drop. My nerves were still raw after answering 20 questions from the investigating detective on Amina's case who didn't seem to think this was an inappropriate time to interrogate me for almost 30 minutes. I'm sure I wasn't much help to him since I hadn't heard anything that wasn't apparent by her injuries and I didn't know of any reason someone would want to hurt her. The only suggested culprits I could offer were the targets of the clients she lured into exposure for her P.I. job.

The loud murmurs of people talking, whining and shuffling about the ER waiting room was the main thing keeping me awake as I rubbed my tired eyes with the back of my hand and rolled my eyes at Brent's face flashing across my cell phone screen while it vibrated in my hand. I took a deep breath and grimaced at the ache in my side that had become a constant since my fight with Vanessa earlier and turned toward my mother whose hand was on my shoulder.

"You okay honey?" she asked looking concerned as I allowed my hair to fall further into my face.

The worrisome look in her hazel eyes while she peered at me through fly away strands of her salt and pepper bangs hurt my heart.

"I'm fine mom. Just tired."

"She's gonna be alright," she told me with a unconvincing smile. "I don't know where your sister is. I called her and left a message over an hour ago. I swear that girl is so self-centered."

"As always," I mumbled.

"What..." she started to ask with a head tilt and a tight expression on her cocoa face just as a mulatto looking doctor wearing thin wire rimmed glasses and carrying a tablet entered the waiting room calling for the family of Amina Douglas.

"Here," my Aunt Pam said leaping from her seat beside my mom and I and approaching him desperately. Stuffing my cell into my back pocket, my mother and I joined her just as my cousin Tamika, Amina's brother Mark and his girlfriend Dana also surrounded the doctor. The doctor's blank expression made me nervous and I immediately feared the worst.

"I'm her mother. How is she? Can we see her?" Aunt Pam continued grasping the strap of her shoulder bag like a lifeline and getting in the doctor's personal space with worry etched on her face.

"Hello. I... I'm Dr. Benton. If you all will follow me into this room here, I'll go ahead and give you an update on Amina's condition," he said ushering us into a small room just off of the hallway.

When we were all inside, he shut the door softly and glanced down at his tablet before speaking.

"Is my baby okay? Why you gotta bring us in another room to talk? On TV you just tell folks what's going on in front of everybody unless you have some really bad news. Oh Lord please tell me she's not...dead..." my aunt rambled frantically as Mark wrapped his arms around her in anticipation of the pending news.

"No ma'am she hasn't passed away. She did require surgery; however, so she's in the recovery room right now. Once she's cleared and fully checked-in, we'll move her to a room in the main hospital so that you will be able to see her."

"Thank you, Jesus," my mom said clutching her chest as I too let out a sigh of relief.

The officer on the scene hadn't been able to tell me much about anything while he had me on the line except that she had been shot and that she was not conscious when he arrived. I'd thrown on a T-shirt and jeans while dialing my mom to tell her what was going on before jumping in my truck and dashing through the streets of Atlanta like I had sirens on my roof. I was a blubbering mess, swerving around too slow drivers and cursing every red light. My mother took on the task of calling my aunt and the rest of the family thank God; because I was not prepared to.

"So, the surgery went well? She's okay?" Mark asked.

"Yes. I'm optimistic about her recovery at this point. She was brought in with 2 gunshot wounds. One in her right side and one in her lower back which was her most dangerous injury."

"Oh my God she's not gonna be paralyzed, is she?" Tamika quizzed with wide eyes and acrylic nails pressed to her cheek.

My aunt shot her a 'don't you put that on my baby' look and Tamika's eyes dropped shamefully.

"At this point it is too early to rule anything out. We won't know the exact extent of the damage until she's awake and we can test her mobility. The bullet in her back lodged between the vertebrae in her thoracic cord. That's in her lower spine," he advised demonstrating by placing his hand in the area on his back. "We removed the bullet but there was a fracture to her T12 vertebrae. That's a very delicate area and some hematomas were noted, but we were thankfully able to eliminate them with little to no complications."

"What are hematomas?" I asked cupping my mouth.

They sounded like some kind of cancers to me.

"They're masses of blood that accumulated around the cord at the point of entry. Luckily the bullet didn't splinter and there was no fragmentation. We have been able to relieve the pressure on her cord created by the hematomas and do some repair to the damaged vertebrae. Unfortunately, we won't know how well she's fared after surgery until the swelling subsides and we can better evaluate her."

"And those are her only injuries, right?" my mom asked shoulder to shoulder with my aunt.

He looked down at the tablet again with a crease in his forehead and swiped the screen as my cell began to vibrate loudly. Everybody but the doctor looked at me and I quickly silenced it in my pocket.

"Well, Amina also sustained a hairline fracture to her nose. Most likely from the fall during or after the incident since she was unconscious when the EMT's arrived. As a result, she has bruises under her eyes, which is common for this type of injury, so her nose and face are swollen. Most fractured noses heal naturally in 2 to 3 weeks. Otherwise, she appears to be out of the woods for anything life threatening at this point," he said as his eyes lingered on me momentarily and then darted back to my aunt Pam.

"What about the other bullet?" Tamika asked craning her neck between my mom and aunt.

Dr. Benton adjusted his glasses on the bridge of his nose and gave a soothing smile.

"The other wound on her side was a through and through so we didn't have to remove it. It was essentially a flesh wound from a small caliber weapon. Had she maybe been an inch or two to her left, it probably would've missed her altogether. We were able to stitch up the entry and exit wounds there so though she will still experience pain, there shouldn't be any complications with the healing process with proper care."

"I can't believe somebody shot her," Mark seemed to be saying more to himself than to anyone else.

"I know baby," Dana consoled rubbing his back.

Naturally, as Amina's older brother, he was always trying to be her protector and his inability to do anything here was visibly eating him up the way he continually wrung his hands and blew out breaths. Mark's father was a rolling stone that I'd never met before, and Aunt Pam divorced Amina's when we were toddlers. Mark's only 3 years older than Amina but he's been looking out for her like a father would since childhood; despite her being a full inch taller than him and my dad and uncle helping to raise them.

"Okay. Are there any other questions I can answer for you before I bring you back out into the waiting area?"

"When can we see her?" Aunt Pam asked.

He glanced at his watch, "Our front desk staff will let you know once Amina has been checked into a room where she can have visitors. It's really early in the morning so of course, visiting hours ended a long time ago but they might allow you a few moments to see her briefly once she's moved. Keep in mind that she is highly medicated and might be extremely groggy if she awakes at all in the next few hours, so it may be best to let her sleep and come back later in the morning."

"How long will that take? For them to move her I mean?" My mom asked as our clan followed behind the doctor who'd opened the door politely escorting us out.

"Unfortunately, that's not something I would know. It's a matter of the hospital having an open bed for her to move into. It could be a

15-minute wait, or it could be an hour or more," he answered apologetically finding my face to stare at again and smiling.

I hoped he wasn't flirting because this was not only an inappropriate time, but I wasn't the least bit interested in him or any other dick carrying member of his species for the time being. When he bid us ado, we scattered trying to find seats in the semi-crowded waiting room. I was exhausted and sore and really just wanted to lay down.

The expression on Tamika's medium brown face mirrored the melancholy one on mine as we walked past the row my mom and aunt found seats in to find our own. Whipping her waist length Senegalese twists around one shoulder, she sashayed passed an angry looking Asian lady who sucked her teeth and snatched her pocketbook from the seat Tamika sat in without concern.

"Thank you," Tamika said with a smirk sitting down and straightening her long shirt over her leggings.

At 5'6", she carried her plus sized hips with confidence and an attitude about it that I always admired...though I didn't exactly admire the extra weight. She reminds me of a darker and thicker version of Deelishis from Flavor of Love season one except Tamika's curves aren't as toned due to the 3 kids she's birthed. Thanks to Amina, I found it hard to look at nearly anyone anymore without thinking of who their celebrity twin might be. Amina says, 'Everybody looks like somebody famous' and I was starting to agree.

"How you holding up?" Tamika asked resting a comforting hand on my knee as I sat in the empty seat on the other side of her.

I shrugged and fidgeted with my fingers. Even though Tamika is my paternal cousin and Aunt Pam is my mom's sister, Tamika and her sisters spent so much time over our house along with Mark and Amina while growing up that we were more like siblings than cousins. My dad's brother Jerry is Tamika, Yasmin and Nicky's father. Their mom was a flight attendant, so she traveled a lot and my uncle, not knowing how to handle 3 little girls alone, ended up at our house almost daily.

Aunt Pam, Mark and Amina lived right next door, so it only made sense that we'd become tight.

"Girl I was shocked. I would've been here sooner, but I had to call Nicky over to watch the boys since Kamari is over a friend's house and you know she was pissed because she wanted to come with me too. I don't know where Dub's ass is. Nigga ain't been answering my calls and I haven't seen him since he came by the shop at like 3 this afternoon," she huffed pursing her cherry red lips and stroking her cascading hair.

I just side eyed her in silence because she knew I didn't care for her drug dealing baby daddy any more than the rest of the family did and I damn sure wasn't surprised to hear he'd been MIA all day. Noticing my look, she sucked her teeth and rolled her neck.

"Don't even start Val. I don't even want to hear it."

"I didn't say anything," I replied palms up.

"Yeah, yeah, whatever. So what's up with all of this?" she asked waving a hand over me.

I looked down at myself, then back up at her, "What?"

"Your shirt is on backwards, your eyes are all puffy, your neck is scratched up and your lip is busted," she answered leaning in taking my chin between 2 fingers and inspecting my face before I pulled back. "You been in a fight?"

"Oh. I was rushing to get here so I just threw on something fast and I guess I wasn't really paying attention," I answered pulling my collar from my chest and looking down to see the label staring back at me.

Embarrassed, I slipped my arms inside my shirt and turned it around until the Nike logo was facing the front. She watched me with amusement as I poked my arms back out the sleeves and self-consciously finger combed my wild hair folding my bottom lip under. Since no one else brought up my disheveled appearance, I'd assumed I hadn't looked that bad. I guess I was wrong.

"So, were you in a fight?" she probed impatiently looking two rows over at my mom and aunt who were busy in conversation and whispering. "Did Brent hit you?"

"Noooo...I mean...well no. I had a fight with Vanessa," I told her quietly dropping my eyes back to my now bare ring finger.

I hadn't taken my engagement ring off for anything since I got it and now my hand felt empty. After what had happened between us, Vanessa's name tasted like vinegar in my mouth and I hoped she was carrying around visible evidence of our fight too. I didn't exactly want to recap everything there in the waiting room, but I wasn't going to lie about what happened. I wasn't the one who'd done anything wrong, so I didn't need to cover for that bitch. Tamika cocked her head and looked at me like a long division problem. No doubt because me physically fighting, especially with my sister, was as foreign to her as Chinese arithmetic.

"Say what now? For-what?" she asked contorting her face.

"Because..." I inhaled and spoke meekly. "I caught Brent eating her out."

I expected a dramatic reaction, but she was quiet. Nothing? Okay so I knew her and Vanessa were closer than she and I but damn. I thought there was an unspoken code that relatives shouldn't sleep with each other's men. I looked up agitated at her lack of response to see her gazing over my shoulder with her face scrunched up looking disturbed.

"Tamika? Did you hear what I said?" I questioned annoyed.

I mean I know we were here to see about Amina but still...I thought my situation was a shocker too.

"Uh, yeah. I mean, no. What?" she said still staring past me preoccupied.

"What are you looking at?" I asked shifting my body to get a full view from her angle.

"What the..." she said getting up and blowing past me knocking the legs of the evil faced Asian lady in route.

The lady cursed her in her native language and said something to me in an equally upset tone. I stood clutching my throat watching Tamika storm over to the 2 familiar figures as one was leaving and the other headed toward the ER check-in desk. Her neck was already snaking, arms flailing and fingers pointing when she reached them.

"Is that Yasmin?" my cousin Mark said starling me from behind.

"Boy!" I yelped lightly slapping him on the shoulder.

"Sorry," he said slightly grinning. "But did they just come here together?"

"I don't know," I told him turning back to watch Tamika as she argued with Dub while Yasmin stared on wide-eyed.

{ 6 }

Yasmin

When my sister popped up snapping her neck, tossing her weight around and talking loud... I felt like the walls were slowly closing in on me.

"...and then I look up to see you with your arms around my sister? Nigga what the fuck is that about?" she was ranting with her hands in Dwayne's face while I stood holding a ball of gauze to my head and practically hyperventilating.

She was clearly not injured so why was she at the ER? I prayed God my nephews were okay and slipped in a prayer that Malik wasn't here too with it or else all of my cards were going to come crumbling down. Tonight! Besides the fact that she outweighed me by 40 to 50 lbs, my sister is a hood rat and if she found out what was going on, she'd drag my ass all up and down this hospital before I got a chance to throw a punch and I knew it. Hell, I'm a lawyer not a fighter. While I spent my time in my books and watching movies, my fast ass sister had been the one running the streets with her ghetto friends, fighting, having sex and smoking weed like she grew up in the projects instead of in a middle-class household with me and Nicky. I'm too classy to resort to low-life forms of dealing with aggression.

My mom died of lung cancer just before Tamika turned 19 and since my dad had pretty much dropped the reigns on us while he dealt with his grief, she went buck wild. Val went off to New York for school around the same time and the tight bond that me, Val, Vanessa and Amina shared had changed. Vanessa and Amina seemed to sprout into womanhood instantly and though I wasn't a late bloomer, I wasn't boy crazy like they were either. Suddenly they were ditching me to hang with Tamika and her crew of delinquent friends despite her being 4 years older than us and I was left to babysit Nicky. Once my dad and her little minions found out Tamika was pregnant by a married man though...my cousin's hang time with her got cut considerably. Now 3 babies later, she's matured some, but my sister is fierce with her hands and I was already injured.

"Are you crazy? I don't know what you think you saw but that wasn't it. If you haven't noticed..." I told her removing the gauze from my gash to show her. "I'm hurt. What are you doing here anyway? Are the boys okay?" I questioned interrupting her tantrum making sure to sound appalled by her accusations as more excuses churned in my brain.

Blinking her too long fake lashes at me rapidly, she screwed her face up even more and turned her wrath on me.

"What am I doing here? I texted and called you about it hours ago. But I guess you were too busy..." she said looking me up and down, then cutting her eyes at Dwayne before looking back to me. "...to see it. How'd you hurt your head? Did Dub go upside your head like he did me last week when I hacked into his FB?"

"Ma'am, you're gonna have to lower your voice," a pie faced white lady in scrubs called out from behind the front desk.

Tamika rolled her eyes and waved the lady off still shooting daggers at me.

"You're ridiculous," I said to her glancing at Dwayne who was now glaring at Tamika.

I was genuinely shocked to hear that he'd put hands on her but then I thought she was probably exaggerating for dramatic effect. He probably just pushed her trying to keep her off his phone or something and she was acting like he'd clocked her. Even when I genuinely disliked him, it wasn't with any thoughts that he'd been violent towards my sister.

"Mika shut yo' ignant' ass up. You the violent one and yo' ass had no business on my shit. Look for somethin' and you gonna find it," Dwayne snarled stepping closer to her and staring down into her face...which actually seemed to contradict his words.

She stared defiantly back at him and yelled some other mess, but my attention switched to Val and Mark emerging from the waiting room by then. Oh my God was our whole family tree here? Who was in the ER? God please don't let it be my daddy or Nicky!

"Who's in the ER?" I questioned Val who looked like hell with wrinkled clothes and her hair in her face.

"Amina. Somebody shot her in front of her house. We been here for hours but the doctor just came out and said she's in recovery. What happened to your head?" she asked peering at me squinty-eyed like she could see my injury through the gauze.

"Oh my God who would shoot her? Lord...did they catch whoever did it? Why did they shoot her?"

"Nah we don't know who did it or why but that muthafucka will be caught and they'll pay for this. Coward shot her in the back too. I thought you was here to see about her at first till I saw your head and Tamika over here wildin' out. What happened to your head and where's Malik though? I know you didn't come here with him," Mark proclaimed suspiciously looking towards Dwayne.

"No. I got car-jacked. They got my bag and my phone," I said escalating my voice for Tamika's benefit. "One of the officers who took my report was nice enough to drop me off so I wouldn't have ambulance fees on top of everything else. I couldn't even call anybody because I don't have any numbers memorized. I was gonna call the office and leave a message on Malik's line since that's the only number I know off back. Meanwhile Tamika's acting like a total fool, your man was gonna let me use his phone to call you, but he left his phone in the car," I said praying his phone didn't ring at that moment and blow me up.

Truth is, I knew a hell of a lot more numbers by heart than I lead on. Including my father, Malik's and Tamika's numbers, but none of those people were options to call under the circumstances. Now running into my family at the ER was already throwing off my original plan to tell Malik I was too distraught at the scene to call him until the ambulance brought me in. Scratch that. Especially now that Tamika was making such a scene over Dwayne.

It was no secret that Dwayne was not a family favorite and I had been a ringleader in the crusade against him before he got to me about a month ago. I stopped by Tamika's to pick up Niko and Waynie, Tamika's youngest sons for a fun day at Leggo Land but she was running late when I got to her apartment. Her boyfriend was the one who let me in and he was as happy to see me at the door as I was to see him. Not at all.

"They not here," he told me leaving the door open and walking away to plop back down on the living room couch where he was watching basketball and drinking a beer.

The basketball shorts he wore layered another pair of shorts and his boxers, which I could see both because they were all sagging and because he was shirtless. He was always wearing oversized clothes over his tall physique, so I'd never actually noticed what a chiseled body he had beneath them before. His dreads were pulled back into a ponytail and his bare feet dug into the carpet as he leaned forward cheering for one of the teams totally ignoring me.

"Well where are they? I'm supposed to be taking Niko and Waynie to Leggo Land. She said she'd be home by 1," I chastised sauntering into the small apartment they shared in Lithonia after closing the door.

Turning up my nose at the disarray of the place, I stood in the middle of the living room with my bag hanging off my upturned wrist and placed my free hand on my hip. There were toys, shoes and dishes scattered everywhere but where they should've been, and this fool was watching television like he didn't see any of it. My sister was definitely not a good housekeeper but hell he was home more than she was anyway. Couldn't he help? I heard the faint sounds of music blasting from one of the bedrooms down the nearby hall and thought that it must've been Tamika's oldest son Kamari listening to the radio.

When Dwayne didn't answer my question, I cleared my throat and tilted my head with an attitude.

"Hello? Did she tell you I was coming or what's taking her so long?"

"Her client took longer than she thought," he answered taking a swig of his beer without removing his eyes from the television.

It's not like this was the first time he'd given me the cold shoulder and I typically didn't care since he wasn't worth the leather my sneakers were made of; but for some reason I was bothered by it on that day. I mean after all, I am his girlfriend's sister and I was about to take his son out with money he hadn't contributed a dime to. I deserved for him to at least be cordial if not respectful.

"You are so rude. You need to be cleaning up some of this mess since you aren't doing anything important," I spat rolling my eyes. "Is Kamari here?"

He looked me up and down like I was crazy, finished up the beer in his hand and put it down on the table.

"Rude? Yo' bougie ass don't usually say shit to me when you come by here so what you was expectin'? You lucky I even opened the doe' while I'm watchin' this game. This Final Fo' season Shawty. You trippin'," he snickered. "That shit was 'tween you and Mika so she ain't tell me shit 'cept to tell you she was runnin' late because of her client's hair taking longer to do than she thought. If you wanna know if Kamari is here, why don't you go check fo' yo'self? You act like the world is yours already anyway, so jus' do what you do."

"What do you mean I act like the world is mine anyway?" I asked offended and frowning.

"You always talkin' 'bout folks like you got it all figured out and orderin' people around like you somebody's boss. That new haircut must be messin' wit' yo' brain 'cause you don't pay nair a bill 'round here. You ain't been here 5 minutes and you tryin' to run shit in them tight little pants and tank top showin' off your titties like ripe oranges," he said with a smirk scanning me from head to toe the way a fat kid would do a tasty morsel before devouring it.

I was so caught off guard that I couldn't gather my words. He'd never spoken to me like this before. Granted, we only exchanged maybe 10 sentences in the 5 years he'd been with Tamika and we'd never really been alone together before; but if this wasn't blatant flirting, I didn't know what was. Then he said something that definitely jammed what I'd planned to say back down my throat.

"Yo' husband know you outchea' showin' off his goods like that? 'Cause if you was mine...you'd have to go inside and change. Now I see why you always wearing them suits all the time. Tryin' to hide that fatty. You 'bout to get them kids at Leggo Land's daddy's in a lot of trouble lookin' at all that ass. I can see that shit from the front," he continued smiling and licking his lips as he leaned back comfortably on the couch ogling me.

I know I should've been offended...disgusted even by his flagrant disrespect. Especially knowing he's my sister's baby daddy. If it had been my baby sis Nicky, she would've cussed him out until she ran out of breath while dialing Tamika on the phone. But it had been so long since I'd been complimented by a man that even his disrespectful one felt good. I was never really attracted to the thug types and things like grammar, poise, couth and a legal job have always been important to me. Still, his blatant lusting for me and total disregard for what was appropriate was kind of...sexy.

My husband and I had already been at odds for almost a year by then when I found out he had been secretly seeing a woman who was a former client at the firm. He claims they never had sex and that they only talked, went out to eat and kissed once during the 4 encounters I was privy to after going through his phone one evening. Whoever said if you think your man is cheating on you that he probably is knew what they were talking about. My self-esteem was already at its lowest point since we hadn't been having sex regularly anymore and our time apart was more than our time together. A large part of our disconnect was due to my desire to have children and his hesitancy about it. Malik and I had just gotten into a big fight before I left the house because he was supposed to come with me and the boys; but he made plans to golf with friends instead. It may sound stupid but...the attention was like rain to a desert for me.

"You must be out of your mind," I managed trying unsuccessfully not to blush. "That was just...just inappropriate."

He laughed and stood from the couch approaching me with prowess causing me to stumble back a bit when he stepped into my personal space.

"But you liked it," he said lowly flashing his pretty teeth that weren't covered by the gold like I was used to.

"Wh... what are you doing? Get out of my face," I told him turning my head to the side fearing that eye contact might give away the fact that my panties were becoming wet.

"I ain't never notice how sexy you was before Miss Lady. You always so damn mean when you come ova' too. Why you act like that wit' me miss Yasmin?"

"Because I don't like drug dealing thugs around my sister or my nephews," I told him regaining some of my backbone despite the heat I felt building between us.

He grunted.

"That's just my job baby girl. That's not who I am. I take good care of them though don't I? Treat her boys like mines too right? Why that don't matter to you? Why you always so mean? You don't even speak when you see me. I ain't never heard you say so much as a 'What's up Dub' when you see me," he said taking my chin between his fingers and turning my face to look into his dark eyes as he smiled devilishly at me.

I never realized how handsome he was until I was up close like that. His skin was sooo smooth. His lips were so sexy but masculine and even with no shirt on, I could smell whatever cologne he was wearing that day. I was always a sucka for a good smelling man. I know it's no ex-cuse, but I can't even tell you why I was stuck where I stood. I just knew that his touch felt good, his body smelled good and this man looked sooo good to me right then.

"I know your name. I just hate saying it. It sounds so...ridiculous to me," I said just above a whisper.

"Ridiculous?" His eyebrows furrowed in slight amusement. "Why's that?"

"Because it sounds like a drug dealer's name. People know what you do as soon as you're introduced."

That brought out another laugh from him and for some reason I felt stupid. Besides, I needed to stop whatever this was before it went any further and Tamika came home. I started to walk around him, but he grabbed my wrist and pulled me even closer. I looked up into his face and he was looking deeply into my eyes like he wanted to take me right there.

"My uncle nicknamed me Dub. My daddy is Dwayne too so when I was born, they just started callin' me Dub. My occupation is just a coincidence Shawty. But you can call me Dwayne if that'll make you be nicer to me," he told me running the back of his middle finger and index down my cheek.

"I don't know what you think you're doing but..." I started to say before he cut my words off with his mouth on mine.

His tongue danced with mine like synchronized swimmers and my body went limp in his firm grasp as I faded into him. I don't know how long we kissed but it stopped abruptly when the sound of keys turn-ing in the lock interrupted. He left me standing in the middle of the living room and met Tamika and the boys at the door. He scooped Waynie up into his arms and Niko ran to me calling out my name while Tamika riddled off excuses mixed with an apology for being late.

I tried to erase what happened from my mind and dedicate myself to never letting it happen again; but when he called me four days later, I could only make feeble attempts to shut him down. I'd thought about him every night until then and masturbated more than once with him as the focus of my wet dreams. We arranged to meet at a hotel off Panola Rd. the next day and I'd blown off a meeting with a client to make it happen. God forgive me but the sex was so much better than I'd ever had with Malik and my box had been yearning for some attention for months. It was only supposed to be that one time; but once turned into twice, which turned into as many times as we could get it in.

"You left your phone in the car? Get the fuck outta here. You don't go anywhere without that thing on your hip," Tamika said pulling out her phone and swiping her fingers across the screen preparing to call him.

"This jealous shit is outta control Shawty," Dwayne told her shoving both hands into the pockets of his bulky jeans.

Panic guided my breaths as I waited in for my fate to be sealed once the call went through. Val and Mark's eyes were burning holes into Dwayne and I didn't dare look at him again while Tamika's eyes were trained on me. As soon as we all heard the ringing sound over her speaker phone and then it go to his voicemail on the third, her expression tamed.

To say I was relieved would be a drastic understatement. I knew he had his phone on him when we got out of the car so I can only assume he'd changed his ringer to silent while his hands were in his pockets. But that didn't mean we were totally out of the woods. Tamika wasn't above frisking the man if she had to and the look of defeat that engulfed her face was priceless. It's almost like she wanted to prove he was cheating on her.

"You happy now? You act like I left it in the car on purpose. Ol' stupid actin' ass. Always tryin' to play detective," Dwayne told her sighing grilling Mark. "You called me here and I came. I'm here fo' yo' family and you got these mufuckas lookin' at me sideways ova' some shit I didn't do. I'm missin' out on paper fo' this shit though? Nah, not the kid. I'm out Mika. And I ain't comin' home tonight either, so bitch if you wanna. This shit is for the birds. Dead ass," he told her snatching his arm away before her outstretched hand could reach him.

"I'm sorry but if you was in my shoes you would've thought the same thing Dub. You know you would've! You been dodging my calls..." she said dropping her words as his disinterest was undeniable with the hiss he gave her before storming off towards the exit.

Mark mumbled something unkind under his breath and Tamika flung her hair around her back overzealously but her glossy eyes exposed her feelings of embarrassment anyway. Running her tongue over her gums with her mouth closed, she turned to me with a totally different tone than she'd carried moments earlier.

"I... I'm sorry sis," she stuttered. "It's late and he ain't been answering my calls all day. You wasn't answering my calls either. I don't know. I was trippin'."

My aching head reminded me that I'd come to the ER for a reason and I winced pulling the now almost totally soaked gauze away from my wound to look at it and putting it back.

"I need to get this taken care of," I told her about to proceed to the check-in desk just as Vanessa waltzed in through the ER doors.

"What up fam? Why y'all out here? How's Amina?" she said pulling the sunglasses from her face and putting them on top of her head as her ponytail swung in the wind.

Why she was wearing sunglasses in the middle of the night I have no idea but that's how my cousin rolls. Val's face twisted like Vanessa brought in a pound of farts with her. Tamika's face lit up like a Christmas tree out of the blue.

"Oh shit y'all not gonna get to throwing blows again are y'all?" she blurted out looking between Valerie and Vanessa.

"Throwing blows for what?" Mark asked confused.

"Val told me Vanessa's fucking Brent. So there is at least one sister fucking her sister's man," she said seeming satisfied.

My jaw dropped so low you could've swept the floor with it.

"What?" my aunts appeared from nowhere behind me exclaiming in unison.

{ 7 }

Amina

The moans emitting from his drunken lips fell silent as Franco's penis went limp in my hands and felt slack in my mouth. I looked up and saw his zombie like expression and his head tilted upwards against the back of the chair with his mouth agape. Wiping the remnants of him from my mouth, I rose to my feet viewing Franco's flabby body with his swim trunks pulled down around his ankles.

"Franco? You okay baby?" I asked sweetly waving my hand back and forth in front of his face a few times as I peered cautiously down at him.

There was nothing. Not even a blink. My heart was pounding with every step I took towards the living room to retrieve the burner phone tucked in my Louis Vuitton duffle bag. I spotted my bag on the top of the bar and unzipped it, grabbing my jean shorts and the phone out. I pulled my shorts up over my bikini bottoms and slid my feet back into my sneakers by the couch as I called the only number in my contacts.

"Yeah. C'mon," I said into the phone before hanging up

I tossed the phone back inside the bag and retrieving a can of Clorox wipes, a hair tie and latex gloves from it. Sweeping my hair into a high ponytail, I put the gloves on and got to work wiping down every surface I'd touched in Franco's house. Considering I'd only been there a couple of hours, thankfully, I hadn't touched too much anyway. Still, I didn't want any proof of my existence left here for investigation.

I plucked the drink glass I used from the tabletop, washed and dried it, then placed it back behind the bar with the other glasses. When the rapid knock came at the patio door, I trotted over to it and flipped the latch to let my accomplices in.

"We good?" Kevin asked kissing my lips and surprising me as he and Jamie dashed past me.

I assumed the kiss was for Jamie's benefit since she was constantly hitting on me and it was easy to tell that Kevin had grown tired of it. I nodded sliding the door closed behind them and wrung my hands nervously.

"He's in the last bedroom on the right," I told them as they both headed towards it and I followed. I'd never done anything like this before and I was scared shitless doing it now. It was too late to turn back though so all I could do was pray it all went off without a hitch. Kevin and Jamie were also wearing gloves and large duffle bags hung from their shoulders. Kevin made a B-line towards the walk-in closet leaving Jamie in the room with me as I wiped down the chair Franco sat in and shoved the used wipes in my front pocket. Leave nothing behind.

I curled my lip up in disgust watching thick trails of drool run from the corners of Franco's mouth and drip onto his bare chest, disappearing between the patchy tufts of coarse hair. I'd sexed worse for way less before but looking at the sloppy Italian slobbering all over himself still made my skin crawl. The fact that he hadn't blinked at all while I stared at him made me uneasy though. My eyes became fixated on the minute rise and fall of his chest and how frequently it happened. I was told that the drug would only incapacitate him, but I was starting to fear worse.

"Quit daydreaming," Jamie barked behind me making me jump.

"He almost looks dead," I blurted out. What was in that?"

"Oh, now you ask? Ain't no reason to even worry about it now. You already gave it to him," she chuckled glaring at him and then at me skeptically with folded arms. "Did you have to fuck this fat bastard or just blow him?"

I tried to keep a calm demeanor, but she had me shook. Jamie looked like a 5'10", Samoan version of Ronda Rousey. She had thick muscular arms with tattoos sleeved up each of them and her dark hair was braided into 2 long pigtails hanging down her back. She was what I like to refer to as a

"Pat". Somebody that could pass as a man or a woman unless they defined what they were to you themselves. She kept her breasts taped down beneath the multiple layers of black men's tank tops she was wearing, and her camouflaged pants hung low above her combat boots. She was an attractive woman, in a masculine way...but I wasn't into women.

When I didn't respond, she assumed the answer.

"You let that nigga Kevin kiss your lips after you just sucked this butterball off?" she asked laughing.

Kevin had moved so swiftly that I didn't have time to warn him even if I had thought to do so. The plan was for me to do whatever I had to do to get Franco to drink the capsule of liquid they supplied me with earlier and that's what I did.

"I got it done," I said trying not to appear as intimidated as I was.

"It's cool. I ain't gonna say shit to him Beauty Queen," she said look-ing me up and down lustfully with a wink.

"Jack pot!" Kevin hollered poking his head out from the walk-in with a smile engulfing his dark brown face and a stack of money in one hand.

My eyes saucered as I fell in line behind Jamie entering the closet.

"I told y'all! I told y'all!" he exclaimed pointing to the floor where 3 rectangular panels of hardwood had been removed.

A huge dresser had been pushed from against the back wall and sat awkwardly at an angle as I slowly approached resting one hand on it and stared down at more money than I'd ever seen in my life at one time.

"H...how much is that?" I asked in awe.

"I don't know but it's definitely more than we thought he had," Jamie said rubbing her hands together. "Now let's get it and get the fuck outta here," she said opening her duffle bag and beginning to fill it.

I ran back into the living room and grabbed my Louis wishing I hadn't been so fashion conscious when Franco offered to take me out on his boat. I had other no-name bags that were much bigger, but we hadn't expected to find this much money. Once all 3 of our bags were filled to capacity, we continued to stow the stacks wherever else we could manage. Kevin estimated the drop to be 2 or 3 feet deep and the panels he removed were at least 2 feet long.

He was a big guy, tall and wide, standing maybe 6'5" when he wasn't hunching with a Rick Ross build. He wore a neatly trimmed goatee and a low fade with smooth skin that even dermatologists would pray for. Once he'd stuffed as much money as he could into every pocket of his black cargo shorts and around his person, he pulled his long black T-shirt back down over his waist and looked into the empty hole.

Jamie left Kevin and I alone to place the panels back into the floor and returned to help him move the dresser. We slung our respective duffle bags over a shoulder and smiled at each other slyly. We were rich!

It wasn't until I saw Franco's body slumped forward with blood pooling onto the carpet from his forehead that I knew why she'd disappeared. My eyes bucked and I doubled over dry heaving. Nobody was supposed to get hurt!

"Beauty Queen if you throw up in here, you're gonna join him. No DNA," Jamie told me coldly withdrawing a 9-millimeter with a silencer on it from her waistband.

When Kevin shrugged and walked out the room, I knew he'd left his Captain Save A Hoe cape back in Atlanta. I was only brought in on the set up because I fit Franco's type and Kevin knew I'd dabbled in escorting in recent months since he'd driven me and other girls as security on our "dates." I was still green, so my roster was only about 12 dates strong at the time, but during that time, Kevin I got close and hooked up a few times ourselves. Kevin told me that he and Jamie went as far back as high school in Detroit where they were from. In the 5 weeks it took us to organize and execute our plan though, it was obvious that this wasn't the first time either of them had done something like this. Knowing that there'd be no love lost between Kevin and Jamie if she left me casket ready beside Franco, I obliged.

"No... I'm fine," I told her taking deep breaths and standing back up weakly. "I'm fine.

"Let's go then," Jamie snarled waving me towards the doorway with her gun.

I glanced back at Franco and squeezed my eyes shut before hurrying off towards the patio door where a stone-faced Kevin awaited. We rushed out of the house and down to the private dock nestled just below Franco's backyard which harbored his Yacht. Jamie and Kevin had arrived separately in a speedboat while Franco and I were inside his home getting frisky. A short Cuban looking guy Kevin called Mateo was at the helm of their boat wearing an all-white short set, baseball cap and sunglasses.

Mateo took off as soon as we and the duffle bags were safely aboard and seated. The water was already choppy and at the high rate of speed we were traveling, it felt like we were going to hydroplane the entire way to the next shore. Kevin made his way to Mateo despite the rough ride and Jamie's eyes stayed suspiciously glued to whatever conversation went on between the men. I was just concentrating on not throwing up from motion sickness and blocking out the visual of Franco's deceased body.

"Nice glasses!" Jamie yelled to Mateo over the droning sound of the speedboat. "Can I try them on?"

He looked perplexed but took off his glasses and handed them to her with an uneasy smile. She put them on and adjusted them a few times on the bridge of her nose beaming out at the beautiful horizon.

"These are nice!" she told him.

He nodded as she took them off, inspected the lenses a few more seconds then leaned in to hand them back, but they slipped from her grasp.

"Sorry!" she shouted.

He held a hand up signaling that it wasn't a big deal, held on to the edges of the boat which was already jerking due to the high speed and bent down to retrieve them. I watched him reaching as the glasses slid around before he got hold and began to rise.

"Got t—" he started to say just as I was pelted with pieces of scull and blood splatter across my face and bikini top. His body slunk down against the side of the boat as my mouth hung silently agape and I froze staring at the end of the extended silencer on Jamie's 9-millimeter. A metallic smell filled the air and I braced myself expecting to be the next body Jamie's gun caught...but she lowered it.

"Relax Girl! He was a loose end!" Kevin shouted looking over his shoulder at me.

Jamie plucked the glasses from Mateo's hand, wiped his blood from them and put them back on her face as Kevin hung a sharp right causing Mateo's corpse to lurch forward onto my lap.

I couldn't control my screaming.

"Amina! Amina baby!" my mom called shaking me.

I awoke with a jolt and perspiration running down my face like I'd just swam a lap.

"You're having a bad dream," she told me placing her palm on my forehead.

A stubby little nurse rushed in in a panic.

"What's going on?" she probed nearly skidding in on her gum shoes.

"It's okay. She's just having a bad dream," my mother told her. "I got her."

"Miss Douglas are you sure you're alright?" the nurse asked me, standing at the bottom of my bed.

Oh brother. Now why'd she wanna go and do that? My mother does not take kindly to being ignored and as sure as my mother's name is Pamela Douglas, she's gonna let her know about it.

"I'm fine. I was just dreaming. Sorry," I said groggily hoping to diffuse any drama before it started.

"Umm hmm...like I just told her," my mother said with an attitude. "I know my lips were moving when I said it but maybe she doesn't hear so well. I mean I am your mother," she said swiveling her neck around to me but directing her hostility towards the nurse.

"Okay. Just hit the call button if you need anything," the nurse said politely ignoring my mother's rudeness and exiting my room leaving the door open.

"Pamela," I said playfully. "Play nice with others."

"Girl please. I do play nice with others. I just don't play nice with fools."

I couldn't help but to laugh. My mom looks like Tami Roman. You know the chick that used to be married to Kenny Anderson and that was on Basketball Wives always up in somebody's face with her evil self. Yeah my mom looks like her with hazel eyes and everything except she wears her hair in a short curly natural instead of under weaves and wigs. She has a strong personality but she's a total sweetheart once you get to know her. She'd give you the shirt off of her back if you really needed it, but if you're just looking for a new shirt...don't ask. You will get clowned.

My mom has been a single mom for most of my life and she worked hard to make sure that my brother and I didn't suffer because of it. She was a medical biller for Dekalb Medical Hospital for 32 years and worked part time nights at Delta as a ready reserve employee for 6 months each year. She finally retired from her day job in January so now she's got nothing but time on her hands to meddle in everybody's business.

"How long you been here Ma?"

"Maybe a couple of hours. Nurse Rita was here when I came in and she told me you'd just taken your meds. We stood outside your room talking for a little bit and when I came in you were already snoring, so I didn't want to wake you up."

I nodded trying to shake off the old feelings of regret and guilt trying to creep back into my thoughts after having that dream. It's been more than 7 years since I was the reckless, self-centered girl that helped set up Franco Diamati and drove back to Atlanta in my home-girl's Civic with $385K in the trunk.

That was the first and last time I ever did anything remotely like that. I hadn't seen or spoken to Kevin since the day we split up the cash and went our separate ways. But surprisingly, after a little prodding and a lot of promises, Jamie and I ended up in business together here in the A. Look, I'm not proud of what we did, but it was the catalyst to making me the woman that I am now. A woman who's financially secure enough to retire from a career that I was in control of at 29 years old and still sustain my lifestyle for at least the next 20.

"Hi. Is it okay if I come in?" A deep male voice asked from the doorway.

"Ohhhh yeeesss," my mother said flirtatiously looking from him to me. "And who might you be? Because my daughter has yet to mention you to me."

If I didn't already want to jump out the window rather than have him see me with a broken nose and 2 black eyes, I definitely wanted to fall to my death after my mother started acting like she was on thirst patrol.

"Donovan," I nearly choked out as he walked coolly over and handed me a medium sized box tied with ribbon.

"I didn't know what to get you and I didn't want to be cliché. You don't strike me as the type that likes cliché," he said with a smirk that showed a dimple I hadn't noticed before.

As much as I didn't want to, I knew I was blushing. Not that he could tell with my fractured nose causing me to look like a football player out of uniform. What was it about this man?

"Thank you. This is a surprise," I said grinning under my mom's watchful eyes. "How did you know I was in here?"

"Well, it was on the news. And since it happened in the subdivision where I'm working nearly every day, Cassandra told me about it. It was kind of a...a last minute decision. I hope you don't mind me just popping up like this," he replied rubbing his palms together and licking his lips.

"I'm sorry but...who are you again? I'm Pam. Amina's mother," she said extending her limp wrist for a shake which he obliged.

Oh my God, she really needed to quit. I barely knew the man and she was already preparing for interrogation

"Ma..." I admonished. "He's not here to see you."

"I know he's not baby, but if he's here to see you, I need to know who he is. I don't care how old you get, you're still my baby."

Apparently, you're never too old to be embarrassed by your parents either. Luckily, Donovan looked like he was tickled by her probing rather than annoyed...like I was.

"I'm nobody important yet Miss Pam bu—"

"Oh no. Call me Pam. Miss Pam sounds too damn old for someone who looks so young. Only little kids call me Miss Pam," she corrected him.

"Excuse me, Pam," he said glancing at me and winking. "Like I said, I'm nobody important to her yet; but I'm hoping to change that."

Okay so maybe I originally underestimated the brotha's level of game. He was really pouring it on thick. I have to admit that he looked even sexier than he had on our first encounter; donning dark blue True Religion jeans, a red Polo shirt and red Polo sneakers. What really caught my attention was the Versace Italian-Style gold and navy Swiss watch he was wearing. One of my boyfriends was a wealthy watch collector and besides showering me with all types of expensive ones, he showed me how to spot quality when I saw it. That watch ran at least $2300. I was glad to see that he wasn't fashion senseless and thrifty.

"What's in the box?" misses Nosy body pried taking it from my hand and inspecting it.

"Well let's see," I replied snatching it back and rolling my eyes satirically at her. "I swear, I can't with you sometimes."

"So how did you meet? You smell good too. What cologne is that you're wearing?" she continued leaning an elbow on the rail at the top of my bed.

"I'm the builder of her new house. Polo cologne," he answered never breaking his smile and nonchalantly clasping his hands together.

"Ooooh so you like to match your cologne with your clothes and you're a homeowner. Because I know you gotta own your own home if you're building them. I like you already," she told him batting her eyelashes comically.

I had to laugh at my mom. She's so pushy, embarrassing and nosy but I love her. I pulled the ribbon off of the box and opened it to find a large round candle holder with a vanilla scented tea light candle inside.

"The best things in life are the people we love, the places we've been, and the memories we've made along the way," I said reciting the engraved writing on the holder. "Uh...that's very sweet. Thank you."

"Umm hmmm. Deep," my mom said arching a brow at him. "Well...I'm about to go down to the vending machines and see if I can snag one of these doctors roaming the hallways with all this ass," she said kissing my cheek and slapping her own behind.

"We're in Atlanta Ma. They might want all that ass, just not attached to all that vagina," I joked.

"Oh no girl. I want a man who likes fishing, not plumbing."

Donovan and I both cracked up as she departed grabbing her shoulder bag and walking with an exaggerated switch.

"Your mom is a trip," he said sitting in the chair by my bed.

"She is," I said nodding.

"So, how much longer are you going to be in here?"

I shrugged.

"I'm not sure. They say at least 3 or 4 more days. I was in ICU for the first 2 days and I've only been in this room since yesterday. They still want to monitor me and have me continue PT here for a little while longer before they determine if I need outpatient PT or not. I'm just ready to get out of here. I have things to do," I told him setting the candle on the table beside my bed and self-consciously adjusting my blanket over me.

"So, you really are like a Charlie's Angel huh? Shot in the line of duty."

"No," I snickered. "They're still investigating it. But let's not talk about that."

Yes, he was good looking and gave me butterflies and what not but this guy was still a stranger to me and it was way too soon to broach my situation.

"Okay," he said forcing a smile as his eyes studied my face. "I fractured my nose so that's why I look like a swollen raccoon. When I got shot, I fell on my face. I see you staring."

He grinned genuinely while shaking his head sideways.

"You're reading too much into it. I'm just looking at you and wondering why anyone would want to hurt such a beautiful woman. I played football and I've had more than my share of broken noses and arms. Yours actually doesn't look too bad. If I saw you out at the club I would still wanna smash. Especially with your hair in those pigtails. Sexy," he told me with hooded eyes.

"Whaaat? Ohhh, no you didn't...ah ah ah!" I yelped when smiling too hard quickly resulted in a shooting pain through my scrunched-up nose. "See now you got me hurting myself laughing at your stupidity."

He rubbed a finger across his bottom lip chuckling at me.

"Oh man I'm sorry. But that's what you get for trying to hurt my feelings the first time we talked. Payback."

"I didn't try to hurt your feelings. I was just being honest. 'I'm better now that I'm talking to you'," I mocked.

"Yeah, well...you might have had a brotha a little bit nervous. You're really not all that approachable you know Miss Amina. At least not when your nose isn't all mangled," he clowned me again laughing hard. "Nah I'm just kidding. Sort of. But hey I made you laugh right?"

"You made you laugh," I said with a phony pout stroking my ponytail nervously. "So, you just came up here to talk crazy to me then?"

"Not at all. I came up here to get to know my future girlfriend better."

"Girlfriend? Honey I am a woman and I'm not going to be anybody's girlfriend," I told him haughtily.

He beamed.

{ **8** }

Vanessa

"Okay baby...well she's here now so let me go and I'll see you when you get here...ha-ha-very funny. That's not gonna happen anymore," Delia said into the phone as she stirred something that smelled enticing to my nose but looked a mess in the large pot. "Umm hmm, I bet you do, but we don't do that anymore so you can forget that buddy. At least not with her...and bring me home some ice cream...I love you too," she cackled scraping my nerves like nails to a chalkboard while motioning for me to sit at the breakfast bar.

Obliging, I took in the colorful mosaic tiles, granite counter tops, stainless steel appliances and glass door refrigerator while sitting daintily and placing my purse down. She kept talking and I kept a pleasant expression on my face while I secretly seethed inside. There was a time when Delia was more like a sister to me than the bougie, boring, bitch I once shared a womb with. But these days she'd become more of an obstacle for me than an ally, and I have no problem crushing anyone trying to block my blessings.

She finished her call and strutted over wearing a grin phonier than the double D's that barely moved beneath her tight plunging neckline dress. The left side slit went mid-thigh up her 5'7" frame and her dark waist length hair swayed with her hips as the heels of her blush Valentino pumps clicked across the hardwood floor. Classy outfit for a pregnant chick huh?

Before her surgical enhancements, Delia had the typical features associated with the J.Lo's and Michelle Rodriguez types; long, curly, black-hair and small breasts to match their waist sizes. She's always been very cute but just a few pennies short of the dime I was. Delia's the bubbly and more endearing one out of the few girls I've kicked it with over the years, including me. There was nothing endearing about the backstabbing bitch I was looking at now though, who still resembled Michelle Rodriguez but with a new set of Selma Hayeck sized tits.

"Sorry about that. You know how long-winded he can be. He'll probably be here in about an hour. You're looking good. And I'm loving that jumper," she said embracing me and then sitting on the stool beside me.

"It's Yves Saint Laurent. Did you see the back? It crisscrosses in the back too. But those Valentino pumps you're wearing are everything. I can't believe you're in here cooking dressed up like that. I thought you said y'all had a chef," I said glancing around her large kitchen which was probably bigger than both bedrooms in my place combined.

"Oh girl, we do but my soon to be mother in-law is coming over later to discuss the guest list, and she's critical of everything I don't do myself. I gotta look like Superwoman up in here or else she's got something to say about it. I swear I don't understand how a Puerto Rican woman can be so racist against me for being Dominican. She had the nerve to say to him in front of me that she'd already prepared herself for him to marry a black girl but not a Dominican. She doesn't make any sense to me," she complained with an eye roll sweeping her hair across her shoulder like she was in a Tresemmé commercial.

Of course, I cosigned with a head nod, but I really could care less about their battle of the Latina's. And it was more than annoying that she insisted on calling her fiancé by his government name when everybody else called him Brand or Brand Beats. It would be one thing if she knew him since before he was one of the industry's hottest up and coming producer's, but she didn't.

Nobody knows better than I do that sometimes you gotta just look out for yourself; but I'm the one who introduced her to Brand. He wasn't my man, but I was working on it while he was helping me with my singing career. We spent just as much time talking on the phone, in the bed and balling out as we did in the studio. Me being the down ass type of chick I am, I tried to put my best bitch on too; so whenever I went somewhere I knew we could make a come up, I brought Delia with me.

Now I'm no lesbian, but I've played one in a threesome a time or two and when Brand asked if he could have Delia and I together one night at his pool party, I made it happen. The next thing I knew, my so-called best friend, was accepting invitations from him without me and had the audacity to be having Netflix and chill nights with him right under my nose.

I didn't sweat their little rendezvous as long as he didn't neglect me, and he was still supporting my efforts to get out there as an artist, which he was doing wholeheartedly. That all changed though once Delia's time with him started superseding my own and she was showing up with jewelry and new wardrobes in the Midtown apartment we shared bought on his dime. He'd begun taking longer to return my text messages and spending more time in bed with me than wining and dining me like he had been. When I asked him about it, he would just say that he liked her a lot and that he wasn't seeing either of us exclusively. I don't share very well unless the other party is getting less than half, and she seemed to be getting the lion's share.

I'm woman enough to admit that I was jealous...at least to myself. But the next thing I knew, the bitch pulled a trump card on me and got pregnant which wrapped Brand around her slutty little fingers. I introduced them February 2014, she ended up pregnant in December and by New Year's, Brand was down on one knee at the BET New Year's party telling the world he wanted her to be his wife.

That sneaky bitch knows Brand would never have proposed to her if she hadn't gotten pregnant. As much as we used to party together, I know for a fact that every time she's gotten pregnant in the past, it was a calculated move. Oh yeah, Miss Dominican homemaker has been pregnant twice before. Once in high school to blackmail our track coach who was smashing everything that stood still, and once 6 years ago to extort her married sugar daddy till she got something better.

How many kids does Delia have today? Zilch! All courtesy of the abortion clinic. Now she's 4 months pregnant with Brand Beats seed and went from total obscurity to MEDIATAKEOUT'S regular gossip stalk and black-Twitter's latest it girl. Instant celebrity.

"Anyway, I'll show you the house as soon as I finish the Sancocho. Oh my God when you see my closet..." she said running a hand through her hair showing off her engagement ring.

I knew what she was doing. I'd seen all 5 carats of it the day after she got engaged and so did everybody on the internet who follows her IG, Twitter, Facebook or celebrity gossip. This bitch is a real piece of work. She knows that everything she has right now should really be mine and if time runs its course the way I suspect it will...I'll have what she has and even more.

"What the hell is Sancocho? It smells like beef stew or stroganoff or something," I asked craning my neck to get a better view.

"It's traditional Dominican food. Seven meats, potatoes, corn, plantains...it's delicious. My grandmother used to make it all the time, so I called her for the recipe. You know I gotta show my monster in-law I'm gonna be a good cook for her son and grandchild. She keeps making comments like 'Son you can't survive off a pretty face' whenever he, or anybody else compliments me. You know what? I think she's jealous. You know how some mothers are about their sons. I'm just gonna kill her with kindness until she comes around to seeing how fabulous I am for her son," she told me with a sly grin getting up and going back to tend to her food.

I fantasized about taking her pretty little head and shoving it into that boiling pot of innards and vegetables while she stirred and talked. But I digress.

"So, are you going to go to Lamar's funeral tomorrow? Cause if you are you can ride with me and Brandon," she said sympathetically.

"Umm...no I don't think I am. I'm not good with funerals D and you know that. I just saw him that morning and that's how I'd rather remember him instead of lying in a casket. Funeral's creep me out," I told her searching my purse for gum.

"Oh my God I didn't know you saw him the same day. You're lucky that crazy person didn't set the house on fire while you were in there with him. You know Brandon went up to Grady to try to see him Saturday when we heard but...he passed away before he got a chance. Lamar's brother said he had second and third degree burns over something like 50% of his body. They showed his house on the news and that thing was burned to a crisp. He can't even have an open casket. I hope they catch whoever did it because nobody deserves to die like that. Death by fire is a painful way to go."

So, she says. That asshole threatened to leak a sex tape of me and him that I didn't even know he made of us together from over a year ago. No way was I gonna let him disrupt all my hard work and the brand I was trying to build with that kind of bullshit. Everybody who gets their sex tape exposed doesn't end up with Kim Kardashian status and I wasn't gonna let him make me a laughingstock. Served the bastard right for trying to blackmail me into sex just because he got in his feelings about me still seeing Brand after I sat his ass on the bench. Lamar was too gullible to be a blackmailer anyway. I fucked him to sleep that morning and told him I'd be back around midnight if he was up to another round and he bought it hook, line and sinker. Thanks for being home nigga!

The fire was one of the lead stories on the morning news the next day and I got a few phone calls from mutual friends telling me about it so I just pretended to be shocked and upset right along with them. I wasn't scheduled to be in the studio for anything until this coming weekend so other than a few texts, I hadn't spoken to Brand at all since he was supposed to have been traveling.

"True. I wonder what he did though. To make somebody that mad I mean. He was a good guy, but I know he definitely had some women that I knew of in an uproar. Especially his baby momma," I responded woefully placing a piece of gum in my mouth so my chewing would mask the uncontrollable smile emerging on my face.

"I don't know girl, but with the way technology is set up these days, it's only a matter of time before they figure out who did it. Anyway, switching subjects. Were you surprised to hear from me yesterday? I'm kind of shocked you showed up," she told me with a sheepish grin.

"Well, it's been a while so yeah. I can't say we've been on the same page much since you've been engaged but then again, I've been focused on getting my album ready too so, it's all good," I retorted making sure to look as unbothered as humanly possible.

"Van, c'mon girl. You, me and Rachel have been friends since we were teenagers. Now I know we had a little bit of a fall out after I got engaged and we never really talked it out. I spoke to Rachel a couple of days ago and she suggested that we let this water roll under the bridge for the sake of our friendship. So, let's just address the pink elephant in the room because I don't like this rift between us and I miss our sisterhood. I'm over here planning my wedding and I can't even call my best girlfriend to gush about it. I'm excited about my pregnancy and I can't celebrate it with you. You know I would never intentionally do anything to hurt you. I would never have even started dating Brandon seriously if I thought for one minute that you had feelings for him. I mean you were the one who introduced us. But you seemed okay with it and he told me y'all had an arrangement. Want some wine?" she asked grabbing a bottle of Dom from her refrigerator and retrieving 2 glasses from a hanging rack under a cabinet.

I nodded but still regarded her with pursed lips because I wasn't buying her claims of innocently falling into position with him anymore than she would be caught dead buying a knock-off Birkin bag. She knew exactly what she was doing and once she saw how he was showering me with gifts, she wanted to get her feet and pussy wet too.

She must've forgot that we used to do this kind of stuff to other girls all the time. But we weren't supposed to do it to each other. I watched her pour a glass for each of us before handing me one across the bar and taking a sip of the other.

"My doctor said I can still have a glass of wine a day without it hurting the baby," she said guiltily.

I truly gave zero fucks about her baby's health and if I had a choice, the little demon seed would've been flushed down the toilet with the morning after pill 4 months ago. I just took my freshly chewed gum from my mouth and sipped my wine without a care in the world for this reconciliation.

"My mother says I'm probably having a girl since I'm carrying so small but Brandon of course wants a boy," she beamed.

I guess my silence made her uneasy and brought her back to the realization that I might not be as interested in her news as she was, so she got back on topic.

"Anyway, so are you still mad at me? Cause you know I still love you," she stated with pouty lips and doe eyes coming to hug me with her free arm. "We used to be best friends."

"We did. But I didn't think when I brought you in our threesome that you'd start taking the opportunity to see him outside of me. You knew I was dating him, and you knew he was helping me to take my career to another level. So what if we weren't exclusive. You know what kind of time I was spending with him and what kind of money he was spending on me. Before I knew it, he was splitting my time with you. I thought the whole way you slinked your way in was shady," I told her motioning like a snake. "But...what's done is done. You're getting married and having his baby and he's producing my album. I'm over it," I told her crossing one leg over the other and finishing off my wine in one gulp.

Her eyes viewed my empty glass judgmentally as she tapped a manicured nail against her own.

"That is not how it all went down, and you know it Vanessa. I know you'll just as soon slit a bitch's throat than to let her have what you think is yours. Hell, so would I. That's why I checked with you first and let you know he wanted to see more of me without you. You kept stressing how what y'all had was nothing serious and it was more business than personal, so I believed you. Did I know y'all were still fucking? Obviously, but I can't help it if he started to actually fall for me. I didn't plan it like that. You think I knew I was gonna fall in love with him? Because you know I was still thinking about taking Crisco back before Brand and I got wrapped up," she said stirring her pot once more before turning the eye off and facing me.

I rolled my eyes. Crisco was her on again off again boyfriend who played basketball overseas and shared his dick with as many of the women over there that he could against Delia's wishes.

"Delia, you can say what you want to about how everything went down but it was shady. Then even when I tried to roll with it, you just up and moved in with him leaving me hanging for the rest of the lease on our apartment and didn't even lift a finger to call and tell me you got engaged. I found out on social media the same way common strangers did. Is that how best friends are doing each other now?" I asked sarcastically.

"Let's be real now. I wasn't the only one doing shady shit dear. After I told you that me and Brand were exclusive, weeks before I moved out, you started picking fights with me about stupid stuff and some of my things started going missing. Don't act like you're above the petty shit because we both know you're not. I know you didn't think I was gonna keep living with you while you acted like the bitch from hell and were still trying to seduce my man on the side. You wouldn't have put up with that shit and neither was I. It was only a matter of time before we would've gone to blows and I didn't want that with us."

"So, what is it that you want from me right now?" I asked becoming bored with the entire conversation.

I had places to go and people to see. She jerked her neck back as if to say, "Really bitch?" and placed her own wine glass down on the counter before addressing me.

"Okay. I was hoping that this would be going better than this, but it is what it is, I guess. I really love Brand. We're engaged, we're about to be parents, and I don't want any unnecessary bullshit trying to mess things up for us. Lately, the gossip blogs have been coming up with pictures and "sources" that imply that the 2 of you are still fucking or doing something that violates my relationship with him behind my back," her eyes narrowed, and she drew close. Standing directly in front of me. "So, I'm asking you woman to woman. Are you still fucking my man?"

I smiled satirically and swirled a lock of hair that hung over my shoulder from my high ponytail around my index finger.

"What did Brand tell you when you asked him fiancé to fiancée?"

This bitch has some nerve calling me over here to try to put me in a ho's place like she had the authority or the ability to do it. I'm the total package and although Brand isn't in a position to publicly choose me over her right now, he privately chooses me every time we're alone together. She doesn't know him like I do and he doesn't love her like he loves me. The only reason she has a leg up on me at all is because he put a baby in her once while she still had them spread.

I could've popped up pregnant too and competed with this broad with my eyes closed but I'm not about to sabotage my big break to get a man and then spend the rest of my life in his shadow while I play mommy at home. Where they do that at? I'm a star and if shining means that I'll have to play the background in my relationships to get there, I can do that. Brand and I have things in common that she could never relate to or contend with.

We've got our sexual chemistry, our love of music and our home life struggles. Brand isn't a twin, but his older brother gets treated like his shit don't stink the same way Valerie does. His parents never supported him when he told them he wanted to be a producer just like mine ignored my dreams of being a singer. Brand's brother was always the overachiever in school while little brother was up in his room mixing beats and hanging out at the clubs trying to see what the crowds wanted. Honing his craft, you know? But his parents didn't see it that way. All he got was ridicule and encouragement to be more like Bobby.

Well, now his brother Bobby is a Philadelphia congressman; but Brand, Brand is a Grammy nominated producer whose name is on the tip of all the hottest new artist's tongues. He's making 3 times what big brother makes in the blink of an eye and now Brand Beats is gonna be for me what Timbaland was for Missy Elliot and Genuine. Whenever I really need something, he takes care of it and I take care of him. Delia can't relate to him like I can. She comes from a broken home where her mother was left to raise 4 kids in America when her father deserted them and went back to the Dominican Republic without so much as a fuck you. Her grandmother supplemented her missing-in-action-daddy and her mom made her money dancing at strip clubs and laying on her back.

Delia can't relate to Brand's mindset. She's just looking for a come up and at least 18 years of a guaranteed check.

"Don't be cute. He told me that y'all don't get down like that anymore and that everything is just professional now. But, you and I were once really close and I'm hoping that you won't dismiss that over some petty jealousy. So, I'm asking you," she said sternly.

Men like pussy. The sooner women accept that and stop trying to regulate when and how much a man can have, the happier they'll be. If I was in her position, I would care less how many women my man was fucking as long as he kept me in luxury, the ho's he was doing discreet, and protected me from diseases. I don't know why bitches insist on asking questions they don't really want to know the answer to but they always do.

I stood up and grabbed my bag from the bar top and ran a hand over my legs to flatten any wrinkles. It was time for me to bounce before I gave her exactly what she wanted, and Brand had already warned me about saying more than I needed to.

"Delia, girl, you know how this works. I'm single so I don't owe anybody any explanations for who I sleep with. I'm not saying I'm still fucking Brand, but I'm not saying I won't fuck him either if he wants to. Now on that note, I'll let myself out because clearly you didn't call me over here to reconcile our friendship. You called me over here to be childish and see if I was fucking your man instead of dealing with him about that," I told her turning to leave.

She grabbed me firmly by my arm and glared into my eyes as I snatched away from her.

"I had every intention of rebuilding our friendship. But I'm not stupid Vanessa. If you are sleeping with Brandon, then obviously that's not gonna happen. But if I'm wrong, then I'm open to trying to get our friendship back the way it was. Just tell me what it is so I know where you and I stand."

I looked her up and down with disgust. She really thought she was better than me and it was written all over her botoxed face; but I was gonna show her better than I could tell her who was really better.

"Talk to Brand," I advised and spun on my heels through the huge entertainment room and towards the front door.

"My man is never gonna give up his wife and child for a mediocre talented bitch he can replace with one YouTube audition. You just remember who he chose," she bellowed behind me holding up her hand and flashing her ring at me as I halted in my tracks.

"Oh, you got brass balls now? You throwing shots and flashing rings huh? Just be thankful I've been letting you live in this little fantasy world of yours for as long as I have. Because we both know that I could drop some history on Brand that would have him leaving you so fast your head would spin. Play wit' it and watch your media darling reputation spiral into, 'Whose baby is that really?' when I'm done with you," I told her just as the front door opened and the devil himself entered casually looking like money.

Dressed in Givenchy from head to toe, his black and brown shirt hung neatly above his distressed jeans and black, white soled sneakers. The tension was noticeably thick, and his relaxed expression grew perplexed as he saw the scowls on both of our faces. Delia rushed to him dramatically with a painted-on grin and her arms wide open.

"Hey baby," she said breezing past me and pulling his face down to plant a deep kiss on his lips.

"Hey," Brand responded standing to his full height and glancing at me with those same sea-green eyes that gazed into my hazel ones, last week while bringing me to a powerful orgasm. "What's the problem? Y'all looked like y'all were about to throw hands."

"I don't have a problem, but your insecure fiancée does. I suggest you handle that before I have to," I spat opening the door behind him and leaving it open as I strutted to my car.

{ 9 }

Valerie

I was jolted awake by loud banging on my door and multiple rings of my doorbell. My head was already pounding, and I wanted to pound whomever was beating down my door like Michael Myers was chasing them.

"What! Who is it?" I yelled sitting up with nothing but the light from the television illuminating the living room.

"It's Nicky. Open up," she called out in an irritated tone as if I was the one disturbing her.

I sucked my teeth and drug myself to the door, unlocking and slinging it open with an attitude and flopped back down on the couch, burying my face in one of the throw pillows.

"Girl why the hell are you in here in the dark? You trying to save on the electric bill?" Nicky asked flicking on the lamp on the end table and sitting in my black leather armchair.

"I was asleep," I groaned.

"Asleep? It's barely 8:30 pm girl."

There was silence besides the voices on the television and I really wished she'd leave me alone and go home. I didn't want any company and I definitely didn't want a lecture.

"I see you're still trying to drink your problems away," she said shifting my shot glass and vodka bottle around on the table. "This shit is getting pathetic Val. Look at me."

I peeled half of my face from the throw pillow to peek at her with one eye as the glare from the lamp summoned my headache to thump harder. She just shook her head in disappointment and leaned back in the chair folding her arms.

Nicky, is Tamika and Yasmin's bossy, big mouthed little sister and the family busy body. I love her to death and though she's only a few years younger than I am, she used to tag behind me more than anybody else before I went off to New York. As we've gotten older, she's grown into a sassy, slick mouthed go-getter who is much more outgoing than I've ever been or probably will be. But I'm proud of her. When she's not banging on my door like the police, she's a medical assistant for a family practice and an aspiring singer like my sister. When my Aunt Jackie, her mom, passed away, I think her and the girls each took on more mature roles than they should've had to at such young ages, so Nicky's youthful abandon is sometimes offset by arbitrary maturity.

"Whaaat Nicky? I've got a hangover, I bombed my audition and I'm miserable. Let me have my pity party in peace for the love of everything holy!" I whined.

Nicky stared at me with a dumbstruck expression and brushed the long bang that swept across her right eye from her face.

"Aww cuz. I didn't know you had an audition too. When was it? Today?"

"Yeah," I nodded with a sigh now fully taking in her appearance. "You shaved the side of your head?"

"Tamika did it for me this afternoon. You like?" she asked swaying her head from side to side showing me the chin length bob on the right side that gradually blended into a low fade on the left.

Like the majority of my family, Nicky also has bright hazel eyes but hers have more of a slant, courtesy of her mother's Hawaiian heritage. She wore very little make up on her mahogany toned skin except for the heavy eyeliner and light pink eyeshadow which has become her signature leisure look.

"Umm...it fits you. I couldn't see me doing it though."

"Okay so tell me about the audition," she pried leaning on the arm of the chair.

"I had one this morning with Alvin Ailey to see if I was ready to perform back in my old position or any position with the company. I mean I did my best. But I just wasn't myself and my energy...my dancing was off for the first time I can remember since I was a kid. It was almost like having an out of body experience watching myself missing steps. Forgetting choreography. I can't even blame my injury for it either because my ankle wasn't in pain at all. It's like I'm broken, and I don't know how to fix it."

Tears welled in my eyes as I thought about how I'd failed myself and how bleak my future looked without the possibility of dancing in it. Nicky lifted my feet from the bottom of the couch and sat down allowing my legs to drop across her lap.

"I'm sorry boo. I know things seem bad right now but like my father always says, 'Sometimes the life you thought you wanted isn't the life you're supposed to lead.' Maybe it's time for you to pursue another career. You've been so focused on dancing because you've always been great at it but I know that's not all you're capable of. And as far as Vanessa goes. We all know that heffa is a jealous, devious and selfish broad and what goes around will come around on her ass soon enough."

"Well, if you know something else I'm good enough at to make money, you be sure and let me know what that is because I sure as hell don't know. I can't even keep a roof over my head on my own right now. Thank God Amina's letting me move in with her temporarily or I'd be moving out of this place into a box. Do you know how low I feel having to take advantage of her while she's in the hospital trying to heal? Nicky, just let me sit here and wallow in my misery alone. It's the only thing making me happy right now," I plead.

"Ha! Did you just hear yourself? Please. You are not taking advantage of Amina. She would've looked out for you no matter what and besides I heard she bought a big ass mansion, so she's got plenty of room for you. You know there's no way that you'd be living in a box with all of us you have to choose from to come live with. Well, not me because you already know my roommate is a bitch from hell and she'd have a conniption if I let you come stay with me. But you got options. None of this is as bad as it seems, it just looks hopeless right now because it's fresh," she told me sympathetically.

"I'm hopeless, jobless, sister-less, fiancé-less and I'm about to be homeless," I told her putting my face back into the pillow.

"Alright now first off, I'm not gonna keep feeding into your misery by repeating myself. You are not homeless, and you are not sister-less because even though Vanessa ain't shit, me, Tamika, Yasmin and Amina are still your sisters. You know that trick hasn't even been up to see Amina since Mika blew up her spot in the hospital and Aunt Di went in on her right? She's lucky I wasn't up there that night because I would've laid into her trifling ass too. We weren't raised that way and she knows it. No offense but I don't know how she could even stand herself after sleeping with her twin sister's man. Swapping the same bodily fluids back and forth. Yeesh! Isn't that like twincest or something?" she said grimacing and poking out her tongue like she just ate something nauseating.

I laughed into my pillow and tossed my head to the side with a smirk and dampened cheeks.

"Twincest is not a "thing" stupid. Stop making me laugh when I'm grieving the destruction of my life," I told her chuckling.

She smiled back at me and stood up.

"Alright well get up. We're going out tonight and I'm not taking no for an answer. You need to let your hair down, get out of this cramped up apartment and at least get drunk off of drinks a fine young stallion bought you instead of spending your own money on..." she picked up the bottle from my table and read the label. "Whipped cream vodka"

"Chile' please. I am not going out right now. Are you crazy? Do I look like I'm in any condition to go out? Besides, almost everything I own is packed up in boxes except my living room furniture."

She shifted her weight to one leg and indignantly put her hands on her jean covered hips.

"Yeah, you are going. Us Vincent women don't do pity parties and I'm not gonna let you sulk and self-destruct while Vanessa and Brent are out there living their lives to the fullest. Which one of these boxes has your clothes and shoes in them? Are they in your room? Because you are going out with me tonight and you're gonna wear some of those expensive gifts your ex-bastard bought you too," she giggled scanning the labels on the boxes in view and then disappearing into my bedroom.

I laid there wanting to protest further but surprisingly I found myself in agreement with her. I had no idea what Brent was doing, though he'd attempted phone calls and sent me texts every day thus far pleading to talk. He could've been out banging any number of other women in his phone right now for all I knew. But I was sure that Vanessa wasn't losing any sleep over what she'd done to me after the way she unapologetically owned up to her treachery at the hospital. She didn't show an ounce of remorse or a spittle of shame for sleeping with my man or dragging me like some random off the street when she was in the wrong. She stood her ground claiming he pursued her and that I wasn't his type anyway pushing my mother within 2 seconds of slapping the taste from her mouth. Nicky was right. I did need to get out and enjoy myself instead of being Vanessa's doormat and feeling trapped in expectations.

She came back into the room holding up a sleeveless, metallic, bandage dress with a keyhole cut out over the chest and a large cut out in the back.

"Giiirrrrl! You have a Herve Leger dress catching dust bunnies? You should be smacked. You have to wear this tonight. And I saw some platinum, wing caged, high heel, Giuseppe Zanotti's just tossed in a box like they aren't sixteen-hundred-dollar shoes. I didn't know he was lacing you like this. Damn," she said looking befuddled.

"Nicky, I wouldn't know a Giuseppe from a Capezio. Where the hell do I go that I would need all of that overpriced stuff he tried to buy me with? Nowhere. And obviously no matter how much stuff he bought me he still cheated so don't look so impressed with his fashion taste," I huffed getting up and heading to the shower.

"Cheating ain't making this dress no less on fleek," she mumbled under her breath causing me to double back.

"What you say?"

"Nothing," she said grinning. "Go wash your funky butt and stop tweeking like you're about to do something when we both know you're as hard as silly putty. We can get dressed over at my place and I'll get Terry to go out with us so she can drive. She's on some kind of HCG diet so she can't drink alcohol anyway. We gonna turn up!" she hollered prancing around envying my dress.

Thirty minutes later I was hanging up my dress and tossing an overnight bag full of toiletries, underwear and a change of clothes in the backseat of Nicky's metallic blue Lancer. Nicky insisted on placing my shoes neatly in the car herself talking some garbage about how I don't know how to respect them right. I just ignored her foolishness and rode shotgun to her apartment listening to her ramble on about her roommate Terry's shortcomings and the crazy office manager at her job.

"I'm serious Val. Something is off with that lady," she insisted parking in the spot in front of her unit.

"Nothing you've told me about her so far raises any red flags for me. What's her name again? Didn't I meet her before when I met you for lunch? I think you just don't like her," I told her indifferently.

"Greer. Yeah, she was the really light skin one I told you whose husband got murdered by his side-chick."

"Well damn Nicky. Cut the woman some slack. Maybe she's just trying to cope. Didn't you say she's the one who found him? That had to be traumatic for her," I said shivering at the thought. I was really angry at Brent for what he'd done but I couldn't imagine walking in on his dead body.

Nicky shrugged me off and took her purse from my lap.

"Whatever. I'm a good judge of character and that woman is batshit. Grab your stuff," she told me getting out and heading to her firstfloor apartment.

By 11:30, everybody was ready to go. Nicky was dressed in a black, sleeveless, sweetheart-neck, thigh length dress that showed off her petite curves. She paired it with black open-toe sandals, silver bracelets and silver hoop earrings. I wore Nicky's diamond studs, flat ironed my hair bone straight and let her apply light make-up to me with a pink lip. Her roommate Terry is 5'5" or so with big breasts, strawberry-shoulder-length weave and gold studs piercing her cheeks. Those things looked so freaky! She wore a pinstriped cat suit with a black jacket, wedges and big chandelier earrings.

When we arrived at PLATFORM, a new club Nicky swore up and down was the hottest spot, the line was wrapped around the corner and I immediately grilled my cousin.

"I am not waiting on that line. I'm already pushing it by wearing these heels with my ankle and I'm not gonna—" I began my rant from the backseat.

"Girl hush. Nicky does not wait on lines Booboo," she cut me off and Terry chimed in, "I know that's right."

"Why not? Who do you know up here?" I asked.

"Amina's friend Maaco is part owner of it and he told me I could come up anytime when I saw him at the hospital visiting her yesterday," Nicky told me matter of factly and again Terry cosigned, "Ummkay."

My heart immediately started beating like a drum. It couldn't be the same Maaco.

"From Stone Mountain?" I asked.

"I don't know where he's from. Why? You know him? Cause he is fine," Nicky said narrowing her eyes at me playfully.

"Fine isn't the word. Fiiine doesn't even describe him," Terry insisted feeling up her cleavage.

"He's tall. Like 6'2" or 6'3", chiseled with a cinnamon complexion and features like a black Superman."

"And a body I wouldn't mind washing with my tongue? You know him?" Terry said flicking her tongue in and out of her mouth.

"Ewww," Nicky and I said in unison laughing.

"I might. Let's go, before I change my mind," I told her opening my door and scooting out into the muggy air.

They eyed me suspiciously but got out and Nicky stood next to me while Terry paid the machine for parking. At the club, Nicky told the bouncer that she was a guest of Maaco's, he checked with someone via a walkie-talkie and let us all in after slipping green VIP bands on our wrists.

It was a lavish 2 level set up with an open ceiling and a huge chandelier hanging down between the floors allowing you to view some of the patrons leaning against the second-floor railings. The decor was in all red, black and crystal looking statues showcasing the large circular bar which surrounded the dance floor and was the focal part of the club.

The 3 of us made our way to the VIP area on the second level and sat on the over-stuffed white couches overlooking the downstairs dance floor. Within 15 minutes, Nicky and I were already on a turn up because Maaco sent over 3 bottles of various flavored Ciroc's and we made sure not to spare a sip as the night went on. Maaco hadn't made a personal appearance but I was definitely hoping that he would.

At some point, Terry's older sister Courtney and her friend Trixy migrated into our VIP area wearing dresses that stopped just below their coochie's and dancing to every song like dollars were being tossed. At first I was a little icy since they were also drinking up our alcohol but Courtney must've known somebody at the club too because our bottles were replaced as quickly as they were gone. When I heard Trixy call Courtney "Fox" for the third time, I asked Nicky if it was because she looked like Vivica Fox and she told me it was. Come to find out that wasn't the only reason though. Apparently, both of them were strippers at THE MAN TRAP in Buckhead. Courtney's stage name is Black Fox there and per Terry, she's pretty popular. Guess who wasn't surprised?

An hour and 4 drinks later though, I was bosom buddies with the rump shakers while Nicky and I got white girl wasted with them and Terry drank vicariously through us all. Once Drake's new song "Hotline Bling" came on, we were all dancing sloppily and singing at the top of our lungs.

"You used to call me on my cell phone...late night when you neeeed myyyy love. Call me on my cell phone..." I sang loudly holding up my glass of apple Ciroc and sprite swaying to the beat with my eyes closed.

"You really like this song huh?" a man said in my ear startling me and almost making me spill my drink before he caught me.

I spun around ready to cuss the culprit out but was rendered speechless when I saw his gorgeous dark brown eyes peering at me and noticed his broad chest cloaked in a black button up at my eye level.

"Maaco," I said dry mouthed.

"Valerie, not Vanessa, right?" he asked leaning into me.

I just nodded like a dummy in a trance; partially because I was intoxicated by the alcohol and partially because I was intoxicated by him. I hadn't seen Maaco since the summer after I graduated from Juilliard when I stayed in Atlanta before heading back to New York to dance with AA. We'd had a world-wind relationship that we both knew was on a time clock since he was reenlisting in the Air Force and I didn't even want to try at a long-distance relationship. How ironic is that considering I did it with Brent for nearly a year? I knew that Amina worked with a guy named Maaco in her P.I. business, but it never dawned on me that it was my Maaco.

"Gotttt Daaaamn you fine!" Trixy said flinging her multicolored weave to the back and ogling him.

"Sssssss," Courtney hissed at him as some kind of drunken sign of approval while she gyrated her hips to the beat.

"You having fun?" he asked ignoring them and looking me up and down like he wanted to devour my soul.

My once bone straight hair was now damp against the frame of my face and he wiped a wet strand away from my eyes as he gazed into them. Again, I nodded and drank the last of my drink.

"Long time no see. You're looking as lovely as always. For a minute there I thought you were your sister but, she turns up a little differently when she comes in. More like them," he told me gesturing towards Courtney and Trixy. "I'd know you anywhere."

I smiled and took another sip of my drink hoping that he couldn't see me blushing in the club lighting.

"It's a little loud out here and I haven't seen you in a long time. Could I convince you to come talk to me back in my office and catch up for a little while? I promise I won't keep you away too long."

I nervously looked around to see where Nicky and Terry were. Nicky was twerking on some guy just outside of the VIP ropes, Terry was talking to a dude who was watching her boobs and Courtney and Trixy were dancing with each other like they were going to screw later.

"Don't worry, you're gonna be safe with me. They look like they're having a good time. I'll bring you back in one piece," he told me smiling and taking my hands.

I was like a puppet with no will as he led me to Nicky and let her know where he was taking me, then lured me downstairs to a back office. The attraction between us was still evident as he ran his middle finger suggestively up my palm while grasping my hand making goosebumps rise on the back of my neck. I'm sure that the alcohol was suppressing my inhibitions but the fact that I hadn't been touched intimately in almost a month was raising my libido.

The office was smaller than I expected it to be with just a midsized desk, a leather chair, 2 file cabinets and 2 chairs against the wall. I could see a laptop sticking out of a carrying bag leaned up against the inside of the desk, but it was otherwise bare. Once we were inside, Maaco backed me up against the side of the desk and sandwiched me between it and himself.

"So how have you been?" he asked practically dwarfing me while seducing my nose with his cologne.

I looked up into his handsome face and said the first thing that came to mind.

"You look like Henry Simmons. Did anybody ever tell you that? The big guy that's on Marvel Agent's of Shield? I don't remember you being this big. This buff. This chiseled."

His eyebrows went up and he grinned at me in confused amusement.

"You watch Marvel Agent's of Shield?"

I nodded tracing his broad chest with my fingertips and reveling in the feel of his firm muscles.

"You smell sooo good," I told him inhaling deeply.

"Thank you. How much have you had to drink pretty lady? Because you seem to be feeling really nice right now. You want to sit down?" He asked beginning to move away from me to grab a chair. A surge of courage struck my usually timid heart, mobilizing me to grab his shirt and force him back into me.

"No. I don't want to sit down. Unless you meant on your lap. Do you feel that? It's like there's an electricity between us. A magnetism," I flirted boldly.

"I do. We've always had that. But what are you doing here Val? At PLATFORM? This doesn't seem like your kinda scene."

"I'm partying with my cousin and her friend. What's so unusual about that? Do you think I'm so boring that I would never go out to a club? You haven't seen me in 9 years. What would you know about what my scene is? What I like to do?"

"Oh, you'd be surprised what I know about you Ms. Vincent. Just because you haven't stayed in touch with me, that doesn't mean I haven't kept abreast of you. Why aren't you wearing your engagement ring?" he asked quietly taking my left hand in his and rubbing his thumb over my naked ring finger.

I jerked my hand away and immediately tried to get around him. I was out trying to have a good time so that I could forget my troubles for a few hours, and I wasn't about to let his long-lost ass force me to discuss it.

"Wait a minute," he stopped me placing both of his hands on the desk keeping me between his massive arms and pinned against the desk. "Why are you running? I'm not trying to offend you baby. Your cousin Amina talks about you sometimes and she told me you were engaged to one of the Lincoln heirs. But you're not wearing a ring, so I was just...curious. Are you still engaged?"

I sighed and continued looking away from him.

"I'm not. How do you even know my cousin anyway? She never told me she knows you. And can you please move your big strong arms so that I can get the hell out of here and get back to enjoying myself at this party...club...whatever? I came out here to forget about his cheatin' ass. Not talk about him," I said in a huff.

He frowned and lifted my face up to his with his index finger.

"I know her through my sister and I never told her about us because she never mentioned that you had. Anyway, baby girl, I don't know why any man would be foolish enough to jeopardize a future with you for another woman; but he's definitely an idiot for it," he said smiling sweetly. "It was another woman though, right?" he joked causing me to playfully slap his chest.

"Of course!"

"So, you're out here looking like the most beautiful woman in the club but you're really hurting inside huh? Is there anything I can do to make you feel better?" he asked softly placing one hand over my heart with his lips lingering inches from mine.

I was entranced by his gaze and my panties were getting wetter in agreement. I was tired of being the good girl. The moral girl. The predictable girl. For once I wanted to do what I wanted to do and my loins were screaming for attention. I stood on my tippy toes and put my lips on his, gently sucking his bottom lip into my mouth and climbing his top lip with my own. His erection immediately made itself known inside his long dark slacks as his breathing increased as I released him from my kiss.

"Oh..." he sighed looking up at the ceiling before gazing back at me. "You have no idea how much I want you right now. But I don't want to take advantage of you. I've waited so long to see you again and—"

Again, I placed my lips on his and settled my hand against the growing bulge in his pants. His eyes widened with carnal desires and he picked me up by my ass cheeks sitting me on the desk and passionately kissing me. I melted inside his strong arms and my body yearned to feel him inside me. I haven't had many lovers and I've never had a hot and heavy sex session, but I wanted one now. With him.

"Even if I wasn't drunk, I would still want you. I just wouldn't be bold enough to act on it. Maaco I need to be loved right now. I need to be fucked. I promise you I know what I'm doing, and I know what I want," I said reaching my hand around to my back and unzipping my dress.

His visible lust for me made me even more confident because I knew him to be calm, charismatic, suave and mysterious. During our short time together, the women who pursued him were undaunted by my presence and threw themselves at him with abandon. But Maaco was always cool, attentive and collected around me. I never saw him break a sweat...until now. His tongue swept his lower lip lustfully when I let the top of my dress fall past my shoulders exposing my ample breasts.

"Val... baby. I don't want you to have any regrets," Maaco told me rubbing his clean-shaven chin through baited breaths.

"The only regret I'm gonna have is if I throw myself at you and you let me leave here without fucking me the way I know you want to," I said in a sensual whisper.

Since being a prude hadn't worked for me previously, I thought I'd try being sexually vulgar to see where that got me. That was the last invitation he needed before taking my breasts in his hands and letting his tongue glide across my already erect nipples. I moaned as his warm mouth suckled them and circled my areolas with unrestrained vigor. As he did, I hiked my dress up to my hips exposing the black lace thong Nicky insisted I wear with my dress instead of the cotton ones I originally wore that showed my panty lines.

One of his large hands released my breast and led his fingers to the sweet spot between my legs as he unlatched from my nipple and covered my mouth with his. Our tongues made love as I unbuckled his belt and massaged his hardening muscle inside his boxers. We both grunted passionately as he slid my thong over my throbbing pussy and inserted 2 fingers while running his lips up my neck. I worked his pants and boxers over his hips until they fell to the floor exposing all 9" of his thick manhood. I laid back eagerly across his desk arching my hips up to give him full access.

Removing his fingers from massaging my velvet walls, he inserted them one at a time into his mouth and sucked my dripping nectar from them. I'd never been this aroused in my life.

"Umm," he said savoring my taste, lifting my legs over his shoulder and spreading my thighs.

I inhaled deeply in anticipation of what he would do and prayed he'd satisfy the craving I now had for him in the pit of my stomach. I squealed, squirmed and screamed at the pleasure his tongue brought me as it licked my slippery slit and plunged inside to explore my heated walls. He sucked my pulsating pearl with deliberation and trapped my clit in a frenzy of French kisses that forced me to grab his head as I released my orgasm deep into his mouth. My entire body was tingling, and the room appeared to be spinning either from the effects of the alcohol or from my euphoric orgasm.

He lapped at my slit until he'd had his fill and rose between my legs immediately plunging his dick into my sopping wet box.

"Oh Maaco!" I cried out clutching his arms as he pistoned fero-ciously in and out of me causing the desk to rise and fall with each thrust.

"Yee...yee...yees!" I continued exclaiming feeling the urge to cum ris-ing from the depths of my soul.

He wrapped a hand around my waist and lifted me up, holding me above the desk and pumping until he was knocking against the back of my cervix. My pussy quivered as he pounded into my sex gripping both ass cheeks and lifting me up and down with more and more speed.

"Oh...shit...baby...I'm...about to...cum," he muttered with sweat running from his brow and onto his shirt.

I tightened my legs around his waist and buried my face into the crook of his neck, feeling my own orgasm building again. My tongue swirled a trail up to his earlobe and I gently sucked as we clung to each other. Our bodies smacking together with an animalistic intensity. I cried out again when my lower lips pulsated with pleasure, shivering uncontrollably in motion. He was filling me completely as every vein in his shaft bulged out erupting a succession of soldiers inside of me. Gasping, Maaco slowly lowered me down atop his desk and placed soft kisses on my cheeks, lips and forehead.

If this was the kind of sex I was missing out on by holding tight to my virtues, it's no wonder there are so many sluts in the world.

{ **10** }

Yasmin

Tears drenched my face as the plus sign glared at me from the EPT test and I sat bewildered on the edge of the tub. I couldn't believe this was happening. I had mixed emotions of fear and joy because I've wanted a baby for so long, but my hopes of having one naturally were dashed 3 years ago when I was told I had a low ovarian reserve. What that means is that the number of good and young eggs I have are really low, which makes my chances of getting pregnant even lower.

When I was 17, my doctor found 2 small tumors on both sides of my ovaries. I was terrified that they would be cancerous because of my mom and was ecstatic to find out that they were benign. Unfortunately, removal of them caused a lot of complications for me and apparently, a low egg count is one of them. Malik and I started discussing IVF, which he wasn't the biggest proponent of anyway; but once I busted him with those cheat texts...I pumped the brakes on that and all intimacy with him. We've had sex a few times in the months after I found out about his flagrant foul, but the last time was over 4 months ago, and I knew I wasn't that far along yet.

Wiping my eyes, I picked up the test with a gob of tissue and threw it in the trash right next to my future. I knew Malik would doubt paternity as soon as I told him, and I had no idea what Dwayne was going to say. What I did know was that I was going to keep this baby no matter what happened. I just wanted to minimize the damage to my life in the process.

I put in the passcode to my phone and swiped it open; immediately sending off a text.

Me: Hey. We need to talk. It's important. Can you meet me right now?

A few minutes later I got a response.

Dwayne: About what Shawty?

Me: I'd rather discuss in person. Can you meet me?

He didn't reply for another few minutes and I was not only getting anxious, but agitated.

Dwayne: I'm busy right now. Urgent?

Me: Yes! I'll meet you wherever. What's your local?

Dwayne: If you just want to say you not fuckin' wit' a nigga no mo' you don't have to meet me for that. It's all good.

Me: That's not it. If not now, then when can you meet me?

He's a freaking drug dealer for Christ's sake! What could he be doing right now that he's not able to drop and see what I want? He sure had no problem doing it whenever we arranged an afternoon quickie. I stewed as I made up the bed and fluffed the pillows while awaiting his response.

Although I had gone to court for one of my cases on Monday, I hadn't been back to work since the carjacking and I wasn't planning to until next week. Malik had shown some sympathy towards me about the incident but was more than skeptical about the events as I laid them out to him. Luckily, since my family doesn't like him enough to communicate with him unsolicited, he hadn't caught wind of the shenanigans that occurred in the ER waiting room between Tamika, Dwayne and I.

The story as I told it went this way. I was on my way home like I told him I would be when I realized that I had one of Anika's bags mixed in with my own. I gathered that we must've gotten them mixed up when we ate together at the food court. Knowing that she was leaving town the next day, I figured I could drop her bag off at her hotel and still make it home in a reasonable time.

While getting out of my car in the parking deck, I was approached and attacked by a masked man who stole my bag, car keys, jewelry and car after hitting me with his gun. Since my phone was in my bag and my mind was messed up at the time, I couldn't remember anyone's number by heart to call and tell them what happened. The hotel called the police, I made a report and was transported to the ER to get the 5 stitches the gash on my temple required. That was my story, and I was sticking to it until proved otherwise.

Malik, being the predictable skeptic that he is, wasn't so convinced that I couldn't remember anybody's number; including my dad's house number which he's had for over 30 years. I told him that I was too distraught and in pain to think straight which he responded to with a silent nod.

Now, 5 days, 1 rental car and numerous card cancellations later, I was straightening up my house before I had to pick up Kamari and take him to his dentist appointment for Tamika. I swear I spend more time playing mommy to my nephews than she does sometimes.

Dwayne: Meet me in front of COOL CUTS in 15

Looking at his text I rolled my eyes and stepped into my wedges.

"It's about time," I mumbled with a huff.

It took me less than that to arrive at the little plaza where the barber shop he wanted to meet at was located. Stepping out of my corny little rented Ford Fusion, I strutted into the shop wearing high rise jeans, a white baby doll lace top and dark sunglasses. Naturally, all their lustful eyes turned to me when I entered.

"Hey baby. What can I do for you?" a stocky razor bump faced guy cutting a little boy's hair asked with a butter mouthed grin.

"She's here for me folk," Dwayne spoke up from a different barber's chair while his hairline was being edged up.

"Oh. Well have a seat there little momma," bumpy replied.

I was glad that I'd put my glasses on first because the lenses were dark and if he would've seen the stink eye I was giving him, he probably wouldn't have been so nice. I smiled politely but didn't sit.

"Give me a sec," Dwayne continued while texting someone.

The barber cutting his hair regarded me with a loathing expression and adjusted the Dodgers cap on his head. I recognized him from Tamika's house where he was a frequent guest of Dwayne's on the couch for a game of MADDEN or whatever other juvenile games they played. I didn't know why he didn't like me but I could only assume it was because I was Tamika's sister and had previously ignored Dwayne and his friends when I saw them there. I was unbothered by his feelings towards me but uncomfortable with the way he was staring.

After a few more minutes, Dwayne and I walked back out and found an empty spot against the wall near the big glass window to talk.

"So what you got to tell me Shawty?" he asked looking out into the parking lot with his hands in his oversized pockets.

I waited until he made eye contact with me and spoke.

"I'm pregnant and it's not Malik's," I said flatly.

He exhaled and ran a hand over his face.

"I thought you said you couldn't have no kids."

"I didn't think I could. Not without a doctors help anyway," I stated shifting uncomfortably.

I don't know what reaction I was expecting or hoping for but this one didn't seem too positive.

"So, you gonna keep it?"

I sucked in a deep breath and nodded as a tall brown-skin woman with a young boy approached the door.

"Hey Dub," she called with a wave while ushering the child into the shop.

He regarded her with a head nod and turned his attention back to me.

"Damn Shawty. This wasn't supposed to happen. So, what you want me to do? You know our shit is complicated. Yo' nigga know that ain't his baby?" he asked leaning his back against the bricks and resting one foot on it.

"I haven't told him I'm pregnant yet. I just found out a little while before I texted you. We haven't been sleeping together much though, so he'll be suspicious at best if not completely sure it's not his," I said feeling the instant urge to cry but suppressing it.

There was no way I was going to be able to get out of this without Malik finding out I was cheating, and I couldn't stomach the idea of what Tamika would do when she caught wind. I'd already seen a snippet of what was in store for me once my family discovered my wrong doings when Tamika outted Vanessa at the hospital. It wasn't going to be a cake walk.

Not being hypocritical or anything but what Vanessa did was way worse than what I was doing. Valerie's her twin and as virginal as she's been all of these years, that was just downright dirty and conniving to seduce her fiancé away from her. Tamika on the other hand changes men like I change cars and she's had a baby by the last 3. Not saying that I'm right for what I've done, but it was only a matter of time before her relationship with Dwayne runs its course anyway. He's not the marrying kind and she's not the wifing type. I'm sure I'm not the first woman he's cheated on her with and I might not even be the only one he's cheating with right now.

"Well look here...I can't make you do nothin' you don't want to do but...this is gonna start some real shit if you keep it. I can handle whatever's about to happen 'cause I can bounce and get my own spot if I need to and pick my kids up when I want to. You though...you ain't got that choice."

I finally lost the battle with my tears and as a few escaped my eyes and fell to the ground. I needed time to think and time to come up with a way to handle this. I couldn't be more than a month pregnant and it was only my missed cycle that made me check. My period had come consistently almost down to the hour since I started menstruation at 10 years old; so, when it was late this month, I bought a test from CVS.

I wiped the tears from my eyes and readjusted my sunglasses on my face as I checked the time on my watch.

"Well let me go. I gotta go pick up Mari and take him to the dentist for Tamika," I told him clearing the frog from my throat due to crying.

"Aiight then. Keep me posted Shawty," he said embracing me and pecking my forehead. "How's your head," he then questioned eyeing my stitched scar hidden beneath my short bangs.

"It's okay. Still hurts a little but it's okay," I told him stepping off the sidewalk near my car.

He nodded pulling a toothpick from his pants pocket and placing it in his mouth.

"Drive safe then Shawty. We'll talk," he told me going back into the barber shop as I got in my car and started it up.

HAIR TO THE THROWN was only 2 plazas up Peachtree from where COOL CUTS was so I was pulling into a parking spot in front of the salon within minutes.

I was greeted by a medium height dark skin guy wearing a fuchsia scarf around his neck like Speed Racer, hot pink overalls and a sheer black shirt beneath it. I snickered inside at his circus clown fashion and told him I was there to see Tamika.

"Do you have an appointment?" he asked checking the calendar on his computer with pursed lips.

"Raul that's my sister Yasmin. Send her back here," Tamika called heading from the back of the salon to her stylist chair.

"Oh, I'm sorry darling. I didn't recognize you from last time. Go'on ahead back there," he told me with a broad smile flicking his wrist in Tamika's direction.

"Hey girl. I let Kamari walk over to Pizza Hut a few doors down to get something to eat so he should be right back. Thanks for taking him sis. I had a client call me last minute to get her hair done for a mother/son dance at her boy's school this weekend and today was the only day she could get in," Tamika told me while primping her blonde curly weaved hair.

I swear the girl looked different almost every time I saw her. The gray V-neck tunic she wore propped her large breasts up on a pedestal and hung down just over her large black legging covered ass. One thing I can always count on is Tamika in leggings. I'm not sure if it's because she just loves the style or because their stretch fit works better than regular pants, but she wears them ad nauseum.

"It's fine. He hasn't wanted to come when I've gotten the boys lately so this will give me some time to catch up with my nephew. I guess now that he's a teenager, Auntie Yas isn't as cool as she used to be," I joked, and Tamika smiled.

"Hey Ms. Thang," I heard a feminine yet masculine voice call out as I spun around to see Tamika's boss Julian approaching.

"Hey there Julian," I replied embracing him with a big smile.

Julian's a 6' something, tall drink of milk chocolate. His piercing hazel eyes, and smooth skin would entice the panties off of any woman if he wasn't as gay as the guys on that show THE PRANCING ELITES. He was wearing his shoulder length hair in long barrel curls today and wearing a brown fitted button up with skinny jeans and UGG boots.

"I see you've been keeping your hair cut up. I just love it when a woman can pull off a short style. Chile' I'm so sick of all these ug-mugs runnin' around here thinking they're Instagram models because they got a good weave covering their faces. I mean I love taking their money to have them come in my shop so I can slay them for the God's but...some things even Jesus can't fix. You know what I'm saying?" he clowned making me and most of the others in the shop laugh.

Malik and I own a personal injury law firm and when someone ran into the back of Julian's brand-new Mercedes while they were tex-ting and driving some months back, Tamika referred him to us. Julian had already been involved in a highly publicized incident where an ex-lover of his rear-ended him and then shot himself before his eyes. That coupled with the similarities in the way he was hit allowed us to get him a lofty pain and suffering settlement in addition to compensation for his minor injuries. Needless to say, Julian is happy to see my face after I won him all that money.

"Boy you are a trip," I cosigned sitting in Tamika's chair while I waited for Kamari to return.

"So, what's been going on with you Ms. Thang? Mika told me some hooligan stole your ride and clocked you upside your head. Did they catch the little sucka yet? 'Cause chile' if they didn't, I just wish a nigga would try to jack me for my purple people eater and my iPhone 6. Me and my family been through so much that my .22 is like an American Express card to hell for anybody that runs up on me. I don't leave home without it," he told us with a snap pulling out the small caliber weapon from his left UGG.

"Man, that little ass gun ain't gonna do shit to nobody but make them mad. You'd better get a 357 or something," a handsome bald-headed stylist added while primping his client's hair.

"Well Sean, if you're so concerned about me, why don't you take me gun shopping? I forgot that you're a gun connoisseur. Why don't you whip yours out and show us. I'd love for you to show me your tool," Julian said flirtatiously tilting his head with a hand on his hip.

Sean sucked his teeth and straightened his shoulders.

"C'mon man. I told you about that kinda stuff. You gonna have people running around here saying I'm on the DL," the bald cutie protested.

"Hmph. They're doing that already so you might as well let him have his fun," Tamika said leaning over the back of my chair with a smirk.

"They sure are," Raul chimed in while fingering through a magazine.

Kamari walked in with earbuds in his ears and holding a small pizza box as they were talking. My nephew was too cool for school dressed in what I'm sure was the latest fashion in jeans, sneakers and high-end T-shirts. As much as I disapproved, Tamika and Dwayne were intent on keeping the boys in hood fabulous garbs that they'd grow out of or damage long before they got their wears worth. I learned to shut my mouth about it years ago but when I spend money on them, it's not so that they can profile.

"Hey Mari," I greeted him as he approached Tamika and I with budding dreads springing from the top of his head and a hint of a mustache coming in over his lip.

"Sup," he responded with a head gesture.

I shot Tamika a "look at how he just greeted me" look and she just stared blankly like she didn't see the problem.

"You would want to get pizza right before I'm about to take you to the dentist. You want to eat first or take it with you?" I asked him.

"He wants to take it with him because this is a salon hunty, not a kitchen," Julian threw over his shoulder as he exited from the salon floor into an office towards the back.

Kamari rolled his eyes and Tamika snickered.

"I'll just take it with me then I guess," he said in his typical disinterested, 14-year-old voice.

"Okay. Get up Yas. That's my client," Tamika said looking towards the front.

I stood from the seat and turned to her.

"I'm gonna need his insurance card though, right?"

"Oh yeah," she agreed while pulling her pocketbook from a drawer in her stylist's booth and beginning to rummage through it.

"Hey Tamika. I really appreciate you fitting me in," her client said sitting in the chair I'd just vacated and staring at me.

"No problem," Tamika answered still looking for the card.

"That's twice today I've seen you in like 20 minutes," her client said. "Small world."

"Oh, is it?" I asked not realizing that I'd just made one of the biggest mistakes of my life.

"Yeah. I just saw you at COOL CUTS talking to Dub when I took my son to get a haircut. I'm Sandy," she stated reaching a hand out.

Tamika's head snapped up instantly. Her pleasant expression now icy.

"What were you doing over there?" she asked me, placing her pocketbook down and glaring at me.

I was speechless. I hadn't anticipated Tamika finding out about my conversation with Dwayne, so I wasn't prepared to answer.

"Yasmin," she called my name again more menacingly.

"I... I was just..." I stuttered looking from the unwitting snitch and back to Tamika.

"You were just what? What did you have to talk to my man about Yasmin? What!" she asked getting louder and making me jump with the threatening tone she was using.

My brain betrayed me, and I couldn't think of an excuse fast enough to believably answer her question. I backed up a pace or 2 with my mouth agape, prepared to speak whenever the right words could be conjured up.

"She's sleeping with him Ma. I seen them kissing that day she took Niko and Waynie to Lego Land. That's why I told you I didn't want her to take me nowhere," Kamari spat.

If my fight or flight intuition would have kicked in at that moment, I would have fled. As soon as my eyes left Kamari's face they were met head on by a ring adorned fist.

{ 11 }

Amina

I'd had a busy day. My cousin Victor, Valerie and Vanessa's older brother, called me from Cali saying that he would be back in GA this evening to come visit me. He's an auditor for an insurance carrier so he travels a lot and he'd been in California for the last 2 weeks auditing a company. He spent 50% of our conversation going in on how he was gonna kick Brent's ass for sleeping with both of his sisters too.

I kind of hope he doesn't for the simple fact that Brent strikes me as the "call the cops" kind of guy if he gets his ass whooped, but, he would definitely deserve it. Victor and Dean, Brent's brother, have been close since college. It was the tickets that Victor gave to Dean to see Alvin Ailey perform at the MET that facilitated their coupling in the first place.

Victor and the twin's parents also came to see me shortly after my PT session early in the morning for a couple of hours. My Uncle Vernon also travels for work since he's a pharmaceutical rep but it's mostly just around the state of GA. He and my Aunt Diane exhausted the hell out of me with their constant squabbling over every little thing and it only got worse once they got to talking about Vanessa and Valerie. Ohhh boy!

Now my uncle wasn't condoning Vanessa's actions, but he was adamant that the twins are grown and that everybody else should stay out of it unless one of them was in danger. Hell, even I was surprised at him because he was always very protective over his daughters. In fact, I always thought that the reason Valerie was so prudish when it came to dating was because she didn't want to bring home a man that would disappoint her father. Vanessa rarely brought a guy home either, but I attributed that to her dating the types of men who she either couldn't bring to meet her dad or they were already somebody else's man.

Anyway...my aunt disagreed wholeheartedly, and she had no problem saying so at the top of her lungs either, which had already caused the shift nurse to come in and quiet them down more than once.

"Listen Diane, these are both our girls. I don't condone what Vanessa has done and I don't pretend to know why she'd do it, but she's a grown woman and so is Valerie. We can't keep picking sides now. I know Vanessa is no angel, but she must be doing these kinds of things to get attention. We've always kind of favored Valerie over Vanessa because she fell in line with what we expected. Vanessa's different. And I think this sibling rivalry between them is all because she doesn't feel like she gets the same support Valerie does. At least not from us. These are both our girls and I think we owe to them unconditional love no matter—" my uncle was saying with the utmost sincerity on his handsome but wrinkled face before my aunt cut him off.

"Vernon are you crazy? Have you lost your cotton-pickin' mind in your old age? Because I am not about to sit up here and pretend that I am going to be alright with one of my children whoring herself out in order to compete with her sister. This is not how I raised them, and lord only knows whatever else Tom-foolery that child is involved in," she told him with a scowl that said she gave as many damns about his unconditional love for Vanessa as she was giving fucks.

Why they were having this argument in front of me, I have no idea. But by a little after 3 pm, I just wanted them to take the squabble they'd been having for the last half hour to their house instead of in my room. Luckily, they decided to leave of their own volition when my uncle complained about having indigestion and her inability to bend on the subject giving him a headache.

A few random friends visited and called through the day including my mom who told me she'd be up here between 5 and 6 pm. My brother Mark snuck me in 2 Southwestern egg rolls from Chili's and almost gave me a foodgasm right here in the hospital. He knows that my heart beats for those things and this hospital food was certainly not hitting the spot. They are my favorite! Around 5 pm, my cousin Nicky drug herself in to see me after a long night of partying and a full day at work.

I was happy when she told me she'd gotten Valerie to dress up and go out with her and Terry instead of wallowing in her lonely little apartment though. Val had come and sat with me all day Saturday while I was in ICU along with most of my family, but then she went missing Sunday and Monday. Mark stopped by to check on her Monday night and reported back that she was drunk off her ass and looking like a vagabond. I hated to know my cousin was suffering like that at the hands of someone who professed to love her. Brent gets the ultimate douche bag award as far as I'm concerned and Vanessa not visiting is fine by me because she's a double douche.

"She said she was gonna come up here and see you today, but I don't know if she's gonna make it chile'" Nicky was saying with a giggle.

"What's that mean?" I asked half smiling, wanting to be in on the joke too.

"Because I think Maaco broke her back last night and she probably ain't gonna be doing too much walking today at all," she said bringing her hands to her face with a hardy laugh.

My face was totally frozen in confusion.

"What? Valerie slept with a guy she just met? Get the fuck outta here Nicky. No the hell she did not. Valerie sticks to that damn 90-day rule like it's a part of her chromosomes. I mean the man is fine but..." I told her waving off the suggestion.

"Girl what are you talking about just met him? She already knew him. She told me that she dated him for like 3 months the summer after she graduated from Juilliard," she said pronouncing Juilliard haughtily.

I was totally stupefied. Valerie and I were the closest of our cousins and not once did she mention that relationship to me. Yeah, I knew she'd met a guy named Maaco, and his name came up a few times that summer, but she never led on that she'd had anything serious with him at all. I know Maaco isn't that common of a name but it's not that rare of one either. Granted, I was kind of into my own thing at the time and living a little dangerously. Maybe I hadn't spent as much time with her as she'd expected, but still! And what was even crazier to me was that Maaco never mentioned it.

"Do tell," I said dryly.

Nicky looked like she'd regretted putting her foot in her mouth as she nervously rubbed the top of her nose ring.

"What's wrong?"

"Nothing's wrong. I just didn't know about them. Valerie never told me and neither did Maaco," I told her getting in my feelings.

"Well maybe he didn't know our cousin Valerie was the same Valerie he used to date," she said in his defense.

I sucked my teeth and fluffed my pillow behind my head.

"Whatever. So, tell me what happened."

She let out a hesitant breath and looked at me cautiously, but when I gave her the, "c'mon with the story already" face, she continued.

"I went through some of her packed stuff to find her something to wear and the girl had a Herve Leger dress and some Giuseppe's just shoved in a box. And she had other designer stuff in them boxes too. I don't know where Brent was planning to take her, but the bitch was ready to go if she would've ever worn it," Nicky said chuckling.

Sometimes Nicky acts just like Tamika to me. No filter.

"So, I took her back to my place and we got ready over there with Terry. Look how good we looked. We were killing them! Well maybe Terry's wedges weren't but the rest of her outfit was cute," she said showing me a picture of the 3 of them at her apartment on her cellphone.

"Y'all do look pretty," I complimented.

"When we got there, they called Maaco for me and he had them let us in with VIP access. We got a section and he sent over 3 bottles of Ciroc and we mixed drinks with it. I think Val was still half drunk from that binge drinking she's been doing anyway but she turned up with us way more than I expected. Especially after Terry's sister Courtney and her home-girl came up in our VIP."

"Courtney. Isn't she a stripper?"

"Umm hmm and you know they were shaking their assets. But it was fun though. Val was up there twerking with and singing loud as hell too," Nicky snickered. "The next thing I knew, Maaco had her by the hand telling me he was gonna take her back to his office and that they'd be right back. She was following behind him like a drunk puppy."

"Well just because she went back with him, that doesn't mean they had sex," I protested.

She twisted her lips and leaned on her knee with her chin in her hand.

"Amina? You don't think I know the look of a woman who's been fucked up down and sideways? Besides...she told me she did it," she jerked back in her seat like she'd just caught the Holy Ghost and even I clutched my pearls.

"What did she tell you?"

"Well first off, we didn't see them for the rest of the night. I had to have one of the waiters let Maaco know we were looking for Valerie because she left her purse and phone in VIP with us. It was damn near 3 am when we started to shut it down and that girl was MIA. Then when they finally came out, she went from looking like that "ussie" I showed you...to this," she said showing me another picture of Valerie in her cellphone.

Her hair was sweated out and pulled back behind her ears, her lipstick was completely erased, and her eyeliner was either gone or smudged below her eyes. My eyes bulged because with my history, I think I was well qualified to judge what a woman who should be taking the walk of shame looks like.

"I'll tell you what though. Our cousin must've put it on him too because he kept her in his grasp the whole time walking us to our car and he kissed her for a long time before he let her go, looking all dreamy eyed at her too. So, I asked her in the car what happened, and she said they went back to his office, talked, and then he started eating the box!" she hollered and then lowered her voice when she realized how loud she'd gotten. "Oops. My bad. But yeah girl. She said he almost didn't want to do it because he didn't want to take advantage of her, but she wanted it. So, girl he gave it to her. She wouldn't tell me how big the dick was but by the way she was walking...he tried to break her little back."

I was stunned. This sounded more like something Vanessa would do on a night out at the club rather than Valerie. Brent cheating on her must've really messed her up in the head. Now she was ready to go out there and fuck the first thing moving.

"So, did they use condoms?" I questioned.

Nicky thought about it for a moment.

"Uhh, I don't know. I didn't even ask. When we got back to my place I crashed until it was time to get up for work and I left her, Terry and Courtney asleep. Since Terry was off today, she said she'd drive her home later for me."

"Courtney? Why was she there?"

"The girl Trixy she came with picked up some guy and wanted to take him home. Trixy was Courtney's ride so Terry said she could stay with us and she'd take her home in the morning too. Anyway. I'm sleepy as shit girl. I'm about to take myself home and go to bed so I won't be a zombie at work tomorrow. The Office Manager at my job is a crazy bitch on wheels and if I don't get enough sleep, I know I'm gonna end up snapping on her," Nicky told me standing up dressed in red scrubs.

"Alright girl. Well thanks for coming to see me," I said returning her embrace.

"When are you getting out of here? You look fine to me."

I shrugged.

"A few more days. I'm walking way better with less pain too. I just need my freaking face to stop looking all Walking Dead. You know I pride myself on my beauty."

"I know. I know," she said in a humorously exasperated tone as she exited and waved at me behind her.

I exhaled and thought about the news Nicky shared while flipping channels on the television. I was soooo sick of being cooped up in this room and this bed. I needed to get back to my life. I'd been thinking long and hard about who could've, or even would've tried to kill me, and no one came to mind.

I picked up my phone and stared at the blank screen. Truly not wanting to make the call I was about to make but feeling compelled to do it anyway. As I swiped my fingers across the screen and hit the call button on the face of my contact, I closed my eyes and laid back into my pillows.

"Yo yo. What's good Beauty Queen? I thought our business was finished."

"Hey. Umm... yeah it kind of is but I was trying to see if maybe you can help me out with something."

"Hmph. Well now that depends on what it is. Since we're no longer partners, as you made so perfectly clear the last time we talked, I might have to charge you for my services."

"Jamie. Did Maaco tell you what happened?"

"Yeah. He mentioned it to me a couple of days ago. And?" she said coldly.

"Do you know why anybody might want to hurt me?" I asked in almost a whisper.

She cackled and sniffled into the phone.

"Well now I don't know anything about that. You know if I had wanted you erased, I would've used something stronger and done it up close and personal."

I took a deep breath and nervously wiped my forehead.

"I know that. But I thought maybe you might know who would...want me gone. Because I haven't made any enemies that I know of and I don't understand why this happened. I've only been in my new house for a week and whoever did it tried to bury me there."

She took a long time to answer and regretting my call, I was about to tell her that I was sorry for calling and hang up but she finally spoke.

"I don't know Beauty Queen. Maybe it was one of your dates. You know, one of those that you set up without me. Oh yeah. I know you started trying to do business for yourself before and after we stopped dealing with each other. I thought that was pretty foul of you but I wasn't gonna say nothing about it since my pockets wasn't hurting none because of it. But yeah. I knew. So maybe you should start there."

Jamie's been calling me Beauty Queen since the day I met her, and Kevin told her I'd done pageants and modeled before. She'd said, "Yeah you look like a beauty queen type and kinda act sadity like one too."

I didn't actually like the nickname; but she's been using it for so long now that it doesn't faze me anymore. What does phase me is someone trying to kill me. I was just glad to know that Jamie wasn't behind it. Or at least she says she's not. Knowing what she's capable of, if she wanted me dead, I would've been. But I didn't know who else to turn to about this or what other reason anybody would be after me. This was it.

"It was only my last 1 client Jamie. When I told him that I was quitting the business, he didn't want to let me go. He offered to pay me more to date him for 3 months than I would've made in 6 months of dating multiples. When I quit our business, like I said I would, I really did quit. I just kept one client short term. Our last date was Friday night and that's when this happened," I told her meekly.

"Did somebody call the cops about it?" she asked nonchalantly.

I felt like I already knew where this was going but I answered her anyway.

"Yes. But they don't really have any leads yet."

"Tsk Tsk Tsk. Welp, that's the kind of security you bought yourself, when you went into business for yourself Amina. Nobody to watch your back. Nobody to screen your dates. Nobody to help you out when the shit hits the fan. You think you know these people, but you really don't. So...I don't know what exactly you're calling me to do. Maaco says you're doing good. I'm glad to hear it Beauty Queen. But I don't have no more time for you, just like you didn't have no more time for me. Be safe out there," she told me and abruptly hung up the phone.

I rested my cell on my chest and opened my eyes to stare up at the ceiling. Maybe Jamie was right. Maybe it was one of my former clients that did this to me. But why would they? It didn't make any sense at all. Of all the boyfriends on my regular schedule that I had to cancel, only one had an attitude about it and it was very minor. He certainly wasn't angry enough to want me dead.

Alright so let me stop being evasive about what my business has been, mainly because I hate the title it's been given, but you probably figured it out by now anyway. But...for the sake of simplification, I was...an Escort.

All I ever wanted to be was a model or an artist. I envisioned myself walking the catwalks of Milan or having showings of my paintings in art galleries around the world. But that wasn't coming to fruition. I was getting small modeling gigs here and there but the beauty pageants I won cost just as much to enter and prepare for as they would pay off if you won.

It seemed like everybody was taking strides towards their future but me. Val was making a name for herself on the New York dance circuit, Yasmin was entering Georgia State University College of Law, my brother was on a Coca Cola company marketing team and Vanessa was showing up in various local rapper's videos and show cases all around Atlanta. It seemed like everybody but me and Tamika had something going on they could be proud of.

At the time, she was wrapped up with some drug dealing stick up kid who ended up being baby daddy number 2 later on, and my modeling career was moving slow as a sloth. Those piddly coins I was making weren't enough for me to survive off of or even move out of my mom's house. So, when a girl I was modeling at a Courvoisier event with told me that she supported herself as an Escort on the side, I was intrigued.

Michelle was a short, dark chocolate and buxom 22-year-old with green contacts and ass for days. She worked for a company called Mademoiselle Models where they actually did book you on modeling gigs, but they had an escorting division if you were interested also. According to Michelle, a lot of times she was just hired to be the arm candy of some big wig with cash at an event or when they just wanted the company of a gorgeous woman at dinner. Sure, sex was involved on occasion, but not always; and they had all kinds of codes and stuff to let you know what kind of "date" you were going to be going on. The more that the date involved, the more money it cost. When Michelle told me her "boyfriends" as they called them, started off paying $200 an hour just for her time, my jaw dropped.

I was up at that agency the very next day and once they saw my perky DD's, small waist and tight ass all wrapped up in this chocolaty long-legged package, I was in. For our security, we were encouraged to get a driver to watch our back and be the muscle if need be, which of course came from our own cut of the money. Lena, the lady I dealt with at MM recommended Kevin since a lot of the girls used him, so I followed suit. That's how he and I got close and how we ended up discussing a mark that he wanted to hit in Miami.

Kevin's sister was apparently an escort out there and Franco was a top attorney for some of the criminal factions in Miami. He was married with a few kids to an Italian chick but loved black women on the side. He had a few houses in Miami and the one we ended up hitting was the one he used to entertain his "girlfriends", stash the money he was hiding from his wife, and kept in case he ever needed to flee. His mistake was falling in love with Kevin's sister Lala and telling her where his money was while they were drunk one night.

Even though he was in love with her, he still bedded down other escorts from time to time so that was where the set up with me came in. After all of that took place and we went our separate ways, I came back to ATL. Kevin just fell off the face of the earth because I never saw him again; even though he'd told me before the heist that he was gonna come back to Atlanta and play low key for a while in his same position.

I hadn't known Jamie at all before Kevin introduced us but it was evident that she was a lesbian from the door. Especially when she asked if I'd ever let a "real bitch" taste my pussy before. I swear, if you could've seen the look of shock on my face. I'm sure it was comical because I stuttered out a "no" and left the room so fast I was almost running.

She made a lot of not-so-subtle passes at me whenever we were in same company, which I learned to ignore; but Kevin started becoming noticeably irritated by it. I wasn't the least bit interested in women and Kevin wasn't my man anyway, but the 2 of them were constantly vying for my lustful attention and Jamie seemed bothered that I wasn't willing to give her a shot.

A couple of months after I was back in Atlanta, Jamie propositioned me to partner with her in an escorting agency. At first, I wasn't interested. Mainly because she terrified me. But after I heard her out, it seemed like a profitable way for both of us to get our paper up, make our own schedules and live on our own terms.

Surprisingly, she had a P.I. license and wanted to use that business as a cover for our more profitable escorting one while legitimately working as a P.I. I went through the process to get adequate licensing also so that my working as a decoy, or bait for cheating husbands would also be legit. We named it, Femme Fatale Private Investigations, and most of our initial escorting clients were generated through Jamie's connections, because I didn't have any.

Jamie actually was a good PI and on rare occasions, I was used as a decoy to bait a client's cheating mate. Sooo...I really wasn't lying when I told people I was a decoy for a PI company. I just didn't tell them that that wasn't all I did to make a living.

Jamie's high level of connections were more than surprising to me. I had no idea that she used to provide security for celebrities and company Execs when she first got out of the military. She spent 4 years in the Marines and was a MMA fighter for 3. I thought she was just a dyke street thug when Kevin introduced us, but apparently, she was way more than I'd given her credit for.

Over the years, we brought on a few more girls to lighten my load and to diversify what we could offer the clients. I didn't get as much of cut on their profits, but Jamie did. Two years ago, she brought on her brother Maaco as a driver for me and some of the girls since he was in between jobs and he was also ex-military. He and I got kind of close, as some girls and their drivers do; but we were never intimate. Knowing he was Jamie's brother was enough of a deterrent for me and to my surprise, he'd never even made a move.

When I decided to quit the business in its entirety, I let Maaco know and we still planned to keep in touch. The older I was getting, the less appealing it was for me to be at random men's beck and call for cash. Yes, my clients paid upwards of $500 per hour for my time and occasional sexual favors, but I was ready for my time to be mine.

I was traveling a lot to other states and twice to other countries to keep what I did discrete in the city I rested my head in. On a good day I'd profited no less than $12,000 for 24 hours of my time when I traveled and that would be split 70/30 in my favor with Jamie.

My longest standing "boyfriend" Todd, wasn't happy that I was retiring though. All I know is that he's somehow part of the BP gas company enterprise, but he's always been mum about his exact position. Regardless, he's a 50 something, semi-handsome, white man with paper to burn, and he wanted me to help him do it. Todd offered me $275,000 over 3 months to spend 1 week a month with him at his home in Texas and to make myself available to him as requested while in Atlanta for the other 3 weeks each month.

Now I don't know why he chose 3 months; but that was the deal he wanted, and that was the deal I agreed to. We'd had our final dinner together at Bistro Niko on Friday, even though he'd actually made his last payment to me on Thursday. And thank God he had or else the police would've been questioning why I had so much cash on me.

Movement in my peripheral made me look to my right where my Aunt Diane appeared looking white as a sheet.

"Aunt Di?" I called to her confused at why she was back after leaving with my uncle nearly 3 hours prior.

"I thought I'd come sit up here to call everybody where it's not so much noise," she said flatly walking towards the chair beside my bed like a zombie.

"Call everybody for what? What's wrong?"

She turned her glossy gaze towards me and uttered, "It wasn't indigestion. He was...he was having a heart attack. And I was still arguing with him about that damn girl while we were walking to the elevator instead of paying attention to him. When we got down to the car in the parking deck, he said he felt dizzy and didn't want to drive. So, I took the keys from him to drive. I just...I just thought he was mad at me for being so pigheaded and I was mad at him, so I didn't say anything else.

When I got to the on ramp to the highway though, he was looking really bad. Even with his eyes closed. So, I was calling him. 'Vernon. Vernon you okay?' But he didn't answer me, so I did a U-turn the first chance I got off the highway and brought him back here but...but..." she bit her bottom lip as tears not unlike my own began to run down her cheeks.

Her hands started trembling as she held her cellphone in one.

"They used all kinds of machines on him and everything right away, but they couldn't save him. The lady doctor said he might have had "Sudden Cardiac Arrest" while having a heart attack. I...I was just talking to him though. I was just talking to him and now he's...he's dead," my aunt continued, opening the flood gates as animalistic sobs escaped her lips.

{ **12** }

Vanessa

If you're calling my phone, baby girl
Cause your man ain't home, baby girl
You're about to be alone, 'cause I'm rockin' your man's worrrrld
So keep him in the house, unless you wanna lose him
Keep runnin' your mouth, I ain't gonna refuse him
Cause when you're a boss-bitch-like-me-it's that eeeeeasyyyyy
To take your man
Take Take Take
Gimmie Gimmie Gimmie
Take Take Take
Gimmie Gimmie Gimmie

I danced around in the studio playfully popping my booty up against Faze as he sat in his chair playing back the new song "Take your man" I'd just finished recording.

"Ooohhh this is hot though Vix," he told me with a wide grin.

Vixen is my stage name and virtually everybody I deal with in the industry calls me by it instead of Vanessa.

"I know right? Brand said I needed another banger to round off the album and I think this is it. I swear those lyrics just spilled out of me like they were destined for paper."

He stared at me affectionately the way a proud father might. Faze had to be in his 40's but he still looked 30 ish with a low fade, a neatly trimmed mustache and dark eyes that looked like he'd seen a lot over the years. He was the engineer and co-producer for most of my sessions with and without Brand, so we've got almost 2 years of friendship under our belt.

He hadn't answered any of my texts last night or this afternoon and I could only assume it was all thanks due to Delia. I wasn't sweating it though because I knew there'd be days like this so, I was securing my future while she was crying in her pillow.

"Say cheese!" I coaxed Faze as I sat in his lap posing with pouty lips and held my cellphone above us to snap an "ussie."

"What's that for? Your IG?" he asked suddenly doing something engineer like with the controls.

"Everything. IG, FB, Twitter. I like to give the people what they want. You know I have like 16K followers on Twitter and over 24K on Instagram right? Can I give them just a little snippet of what we just recorded?" I pled with pouty lips.

"Nope. Nothing is copy written yet and you'll be the first one pissed off when somebody else comes out with your song on YouTube," he told me as I looked down at my vibrating phone.

Ig-fucking-nore! I don't know what the hell my mother was calling me for earlier before I started my session, and I didn't know what Tamika's instigating ass was calling me for now either; but I didn't care enough to find out. I was in a good head space and I wasn't going to let my petty family problems disrupt that.

"So did Mr. Beats give you an ETA of when he was expected to show up or nah?" I said exaggerating the "nah" playfully as I swept my hair, which included a blend of brown and purple highlighted clip-ins over my back.

He sighed and reclined back in his chair looking at me with hooded eyes as I retrieved a pack of cigs from my pocketbook and a lighter.

"No. He has not. Smoking is not good for your vocal cords Vix. I thought Brand told you to quit those?"

"Brand, is not here though, is he? I'll quit next week before I start the choreography for my performance at Fiya Fest," I told him starting to light my cigarette.

"Don't light that in here. If you're gonna smoke, go outside. You know better than that."

I rolled my eyes and crossed my arms under my breasts which were pertly displayed in a low-cut, pink laced razor-backed top. My Seven jeans were skin-tight, and I could see his eyes taking in the plump shape of my ass in them. Especially since I'd poked it out specifically for his viewing pleasure. Like I said before, I like to give the people what they want.

"Y'all smoke blunts in here all the time so why can't I smoke a cigarette? Every time I light up, somebody got a problem like I'm lighting a stick of dynamite or something. I swear y'all are such hypocrites," I sucked my teeth.

"Go outside and smoke that," he said waving me off more sternly and turning his back to me as he started playing my song again and adjusting volumes.

I grabbed my phone and flung the door open with attitude as I sashayed haughtily down the hall and towards the back-EXIT door leading to where delivery trucks came, and where I normally smoked. I held the loosy between my fingers and squeezed the box of Newports into my back pocket. Lighting it, I took a deep drag and started thumbing through my phone after I posted my pics with the caption, "Boss Bitch handling business in the studio. #TakeYourMan coming soon."

Blowing smoke in the air, I smiled thinking about the fame that was coming my way once my album comes out on Brand's indie label. My rise to the top has been a long time in the making, but I was just starting to feel fame right under my fingertips.

"Fuck you out here smokin' for?" Brand spat busting through the door I had propped open with the designated stick the rest of the smoker's used to do the same thing.

"Umm...because I can. And because you're late," I answered with a sassy smile, happy to see him.

"I told you to stop doing that shit. It's gonna damage your vocal cords and shorten your career longevity," he snarled at me.

"Well hello to you too. Comin' out here all huffy and demanding."

"I came here to work, and your dumb ass is out here smokin' away my time."

"Hold up. First off, you're late. Second off, me and Faze just recorded an entire song that I just wrote yest-er-day. So clearly, I have been productive already. What's your fuckin' problem anyway?" I asked taking another puff before he reached out and slapped it from my fingers.

"Wow. Seriously?" I said looking from my cig on the dirty ground and back to him.

"Quit those fucking cancer sticks Vix," he demanded with his chin in the air as he towered over me.

He was so sexy. I liked it when he was forceful because he knows I don't bow down to men easily. So if you don't take charge, I will control you. I eyed his jeans, throwback Falcon's jersey and red Yeezy's before looking into his dreamy sea-green eyes. I'd never seen eyes so beautiful and magnetic in all my life. I knew we would make beautiful babies too.

I reached my hand out as I neared him and placed one hand on his chest.

"Why you being so mean to me baby? You mad about your baby momma?" I asked slickly.

"I thought I told you not to rattle her cage. You know my situation. That shit you pulled yesterday was not cool, at-all," he retorted glaring down at me. "She called you over there to make amends, but your arrogant ass just had to push her buttons, didn't you? For what reason?"

I sighed and ran my hand down his cheek and over his lips as my eyes followed the trail.

"Because she was trying to check me. I know she's having your baby. At least that's what she says, but-" I was saying before he abruptly grabbed my shoulders.

"Yo! You going too far with this shit Vix. I don't play about my seed. You better cool your mu-fuckin' heels on that. That's my fiancé and the mother of my child. Point blank and a mu-fuckin' period. Don't let me hear you come out of your mouth disrespecting Delia again. Stay in your fuckin' lane," he screamed into my face shaking me.

I was a little startled because he'd never put his hands on me for any reason other than to make me feel good before. I wasn't about to let him know he had me shook so I snapped on him like I would any-body else.

"Get your hands off me!" I screamed back punching him in the chest with both fists causing him to reluctantly release me. "You must've lost your mind. I don't know if Delia lets you do that shit with her...but you ain't about to do that shit with me. This is not how we get down at all. Are you seriously acting this crazy with me over her?"

Like really? The more I thought about it, the more upset I was get-ting. All of the sudden just because she's pregnant she's above every-body else? Fuck outta here! I've been holding him down since before her and I planned to be holding him down way after her.

He was so agitated that he couldn't stand still, and I was beginning to mirror the sentiment as I rubbed my right shoulder.

"Fucking asshole," I said under my breath looking at the reddened area where he'd grabbed me. "You better make sure you even know it's your baby before you're out here fighting for it."

"What?" he asked with narrowed eyes as the glare from the lamp posts illuminating the back gleamed off of his jewelry.

"I said...you better make sure!" I hollered defiantly. "You weren't the only one she was fucking when she got pregnant. Meanwhile you got her up on a pedestal. I've known her way longer than you have, and I know her M.O. and where the bodies are buried."

"Who else was she fucking then?" he asked in an eerily calm manner.

I shrugged and started to head back inside until he once again grabbed my arm forcefully.

"Who else was she fucking?" he grilled me through clenched teeth.

"Get-off-me," I growled struggling to flee his grip to no avail.

"You know what Vix? I should've stopped fuckin' wit' you a long time ago. I thought you were special," he said jabbing the air at me with his free hand while tightening the grip on me with the other. "But you're not. You're just another gold diggin' broad lookin' for a come up any way that you can. I've still been keeping your triflin' ass laced since me and Delia made it official but that's not enough is it? It ain't enough for you. What is it that you want? Huh? What exactly do you want from me besides trying to make you a star? Because I've been doing that and you're still trying to fuck my shit up with Wifey," he asked with fury shimmering in his eyes.

Maybe I'd gone too far this time; but the ego in me wouldn't allow me to humble myself in light of the things he'd just said.

"I wanted you! We had something building before you let your dick get you into something your ass couldn't get out of. What about me? I give you what you want, when you want it, but you're still going home to her every night. Why? Why huh?" I yelled in his face feeling the rage and jealousy I'd been harboring coming to the surface.

"Oh, so it's me you want? It's me you want huh?" he was saying as he shoved me against the building and began trying to unbutton my pants.

I was momentarily frozen. The cold look in his eyes was alarming all of my senses at one time. I started pushing him away from me, but he pinned my back to the wall and held me there with his forearm under my neck.

"Stop!" I cried out struggling under the weight of his arm and his body which was partially pressed against me.

He finally got the buttons on my jeans open and ripped the zipper down with his free hand as I squirmed beneath him. I'd voluntarily given him anything he wanted before. And had he not been so rough with me, I would've been doing the same thing now. But the look in his eyes and the strength he was using to restrain me was nothing short of frightening.

"Stop it Brand! You're hurting me. I'm sorry," I begged with all courage fleeting as I watched him unbuckling his jeans.

His lips were pressed tightly together, and his hands were cold as he yanked at my jeans and panties until they were down to my ankles.

"This is what you want right? This is what you're always thirsting for right?" he murmured snatching me from the wall and then slamming me back up against it face first.

One large hand was gripping the back of my neck as he held my aching forehead pressed against the wall while the other positioned my waist where he wanted it. I could barely catch my breath before I felt him trying to cram his huge dick inside of my dehydrated vagina.

"Brand...please. I'm sorry. Don't do this," I pled with tears now scurrying down my face.

My attempts to buck him off of me from behind were feeble and when I reached one hand up to try and remove his clutch from the back of my neck, he rammed my forehead into the wall harder.

"No. You gonna get what the fuck you want for a change. You're always complaining about what everybody else has that you deserve right? Well, here's what you deserve," he hissed into my ear jerking me at the waist where he had me bent over and shoving a finger wet with his saliva between my legs parting the lips that once invited him to have me anyway he wanted.

"Funny how this shit you brag about always being so gushy ain't gushy right now. What's the matter Vix? You getting more than you wanted?" he mocked as a sharp pain shot through my loins and his manhood violated my entrance.

The pain and humiliation of the assault took the fight out of me and I just decided to let him have his way. The sooner I did, the sooner it would be over. He continued to pump with deep and long strokes, each feeling like it was tearing away at the delicate fabric of my orifice while he grunted and pounded me doggy style.

"This-is-what-you-want," he kept repeating with each thrust.

I didn't recognize the voice of evil uttering those words or the person who was taking without consent, what had previously been given to him freely. I managed to place one hand between my head and the wall just as he drove me into it one last time and fired ropes of semen into my sullied womb.

All at once he withdrew himself and released me, stumbling backwards and panting like a marathon runner. The pure look of satisfaction on his face was evident as I stood with the excess of his seeds drizzling from my burning box and down my inner thigh.

I had no words. My spirit was crushed and my perception of the man who stood before me zipping up his jeans forever impaired.

"Now if you wanna work...let's work. No more of this other bullshit or I'm pulling the plug on your album release for good. What we had is over. It's strictly business from here on out," he told me with his lips contorted into a snarl before jerking the door open and going inside.

I didn't want to move. I just wanted to wake up from this nightmare and see that it had never actually happened. Unfortunately, my painfully throbbing vagina was screaming that it had, and the back of my neck and my forehead ached in agreement. I slowly began pulling my panties and jeans up, realizing I'd never let go of my phone when it vibrated in my hand with my Aunt Pam's face on the screen. I snorted at the comedy of it all, even though there was nothing funny about what had just occurred.

It was the most inopportune moment ever to take a phone call, but I figured, "fuck it."

"Hello?" I answered dryly balancing my cell between my shoulder and my ear.

"Why the hell haven't you been answering your phone girl? Your mother's been trying to get in touch with you for hours," she scolded.

"What?" I asked too exhausted to put up any argument in my defense.

"Where are you? I need you to sit down right now."

"What Aunt Pam? Just say it."

Her voice was quivering, and I thought I heard distraught voices in the background but couldn't tell if it was the television or not. All I knew was that I needed a cigarette to calm my nerves before I did anything else. Just as I'd placed a palm in my back pocket to retrieve my pack of Newports, she spoke.

"Vanessa...baby. Vernon had a heart attack. He didn't make it."

I stumbled against the wall, grasping my throat when the air left my lungs, and everything seemed to be spinning.

"He..." was all I could voice as I slid to the ground and an eruption of tears tailgated my wailing.

{ 13 }

Valerie

"Okay, so I would like the family of the deceased to please stand over here. We'll be ready for your entrance in about 5 minutes. Is everybody that will be sitting in the first 2 pews here already? Or are we still waiting on a couple of folk?" the funeral director asked steering me across the room.

I think it was already clear why we were all there, so there was no need for her to reiterate that she needed the family of the "deceased." But I complied without a word and found an empty chair at a table in the corner to sit in.

"Hey cuz," Nicky said red-eyed departing from the group to stand beside me. "Do you want me to get you some water or something?"

I shook my head no and swallowed hard as I watched everyone shuffle about talking.

She was clearly at a loss of words, but I could see that she wanted to comfort me in whatever way possible. Honestly, I just wanted her, and everybody else to leave me alone but I would never have said it. I caught sight of my mother emerging from the bathroom wiping her eyes with my Aunt Pam close behind her. My mom's hair was curled softly around her face and her make-up had already been partially wiped away.

When Amina told me what happened, I was in disbelief. My dad was only 54 and was in relatively good health. I knew that my mom was feeling a load of guilt on her shoulders and it was easy to see it in her face. Amina said they'd argued listlessly and loudly about what Vanessa did to me while visiting her at the hospital until he started complaining of feeling indigestion.

I was shocked when she said that he'd wanted Vanessa and I to work out our issues without them taking sides. The only side should have been right or wrong and she was obviously in the wrong for what she did to me. The thing I most regretted though was that I hadn't even seen or talked to my father in the last 2 weeks. I knew he'd got the news via my mother, but I didn't reach out to cry on his shoulder and he hadn't called to ask about me.

Although he usually went along with whatever my mother determined was just, I always felt like my father had a soft spot for Vanessa. No matter what type of mess she got into, he always had her back. Of course, he was always supportive of me too, but when I went away, I think he built a stronger bond with her than he had with me.

My mother has always been hardcore about education, etiquette, poise, etc. And I've always tried to embody that as a result of our upbringing; but Vanessa didn't necessarily subscribe to those values. Once I was 650 miles away, I guess she didn't have any incentive to try to maintain them. For some reason, she seems to think my entire life is a breeze and I've never struggled or suffered through anything.

I'm sure most of my family would mirror the sentiment too because I don't wear my feelings and thoughts on my sleeve or verbalize everything that happens in my life. The funny thing is that everybody thinks they're such an expert on me and how I am regardless of the fact that I rarely share my most intimate feelings with any of them.

Amina came home from the hospital the day after my dad died and I was supposed to be moving my stuff into her house the next day, Friday, until I could get my own spot. Well, there was a change of plans Thursday night after she grilled me about Maaco and got in her feelings because I hadn't told her about my relationship with him before. Then, she proceeded to school me on the importance of having safe sex.

Can you freaking believe that? I'll be 30 years old in 2 months and she was coming at me like an after school special about my sex life? Priceless.

After the week I'd had, I was in no mood for hers or anyone else's bullshit. I was starting to feel like everybody thought they could just do and say whatever they wanted to to me and I was supposed to bend or crumble on command. I won't say we argued, but it got more heated than a normal conversation. I felt like she thought she was the all-knowing boss of my life and was being too presumptuous and domineering about my relationship with Maaco.

First of all, I never asked for her input on what I did or didn't do with him but unfortunately, since I was drunk that night, my mouth had run like a faucet when Nicky put me on the witness stand after the club. Frankly, though he'd attempted to call me twice, I hadn't spoken to Maaco at all after that night.

Brent's stupid self was still trying to get me to reconcile and I really wasn't in a place where I wanted to give any man the time of day. I'm glad we went to the club though because I needed to blow off some steam, let down my hair and live my life without boundaries. As it turned out, Courtney's friend ditching her at the club, was a blessing for me because the next morning we were vibing over breakfast and she opened my eyes to something I never thought I'd be interested in. Stripping.

I wasn't really confident that I could get up in front of a crowd of men and sometimes women, and dance while taking my clothes off; but she assured me that the only difference in what I'd done professionally before and what I'd be doing professionally as a stripper was that all eyes would be on me and nobody else. Originally, I was going to run the idea past Amina to see what she thought about it, but I didn't bother after she'd proclaimed herself my guidance counselor without solicitation.

When Friday morning came, I just drove the Uhaul over to my parent's house and cluttered one side of their garage with my dismantled bedroom set, my couch, armchair, and boxes until further notice. My mother was overtly grieving but ecstatic that I was coming to stay with her. She really didn't want to be in the house alone and there were 3 perfectly vacant extra bedrooms in the house.

"Okay so it looks like everyone is here. Yes?" the older black lady, probably in her 50's, asked still directing us and snapping me from my thoughts.

"Yes," Aunt Pam said waving for me to come to the front.

My brother Victor wrapped an arm around my shoulder and pulled me into his strong chest.

"I got you baby sis," he told me planting a kiss on my forehead that soothed a little of the ache in my heart.

Victor's 6 years older than me and has always been a protective big brother to me and Vanessa. Even though his mom is not ours, he spent just as much time at our house as he did at home. Everybody knew that if you wanted to date any of the Vincent twins, big brother Victor was going to be checking for you.

Up ahead was my mother who was standing between my Uncle Jerry, who's Tamika, Yasmin and Nicky's dad, and my Aunt Pam. Speaking of Yasmin, I hadn't seen her at all since the news came out about her and Dub. I swear my family is trifling.

Looking behind me, I saw Nicky standing next to Tamika and her 3 boys, then Mark stood arm and arm with Amina behind them. Vanessa was nowhere in sight and I wasn't really even sure if she was coming. I knew she'd been by to see my mom while I was at the house, but I stayed held up in the room I was staying in until she left. She came to the wake last night, but we didn't speak and barely made eye contact with each other. If anybody was going to break the ice, it should've been her. It damn sure wasn't going to be me.

The organ music played, and the family was led down the aisle between the packed church of mourners. My dad was a quiet man. Some say we were similar in that way, but he was also very loving and level-headed. I could barely look at him lying in the casket at the wake last night and I wasn't doing much better now.

I buried my face into my brother's armpit as anguish began to overwhelm me and we all took our seat on the first row. The rest of the funeral was a blur to me. Both my mom and my uncle Jerry went up to the podium and I know there were a lot of speeches, singing and some laughter; but if you asked me what they said I couldn't tell you.

Afterwards, we all went to the burial site and put my daddy into the ground at Lockwood Cemetery. My mom wept silently with my Aunt rubbing her back as various friends and family members leaned in to give her their condolences and prayers. Most people relayed the same to me and my brother as I sat numb and dazed using him as my crutch.

My attention was drawn when a familiar, muscular man approached dressed in a sleek charcoal-gray suit.

"I just came to pay my condolences to you and your family. Your father was a good man, and he was always—" he was saying before my brother cut him off.

"Man... get your ass outta here. We don't need your fucking condolences and she doesn't need your sympathy," Victor growled at him jumping up from his seat. "You think my father would want the scum bag who was promised to one of his daughters but was fucking both of them to bring his sorry ass condolences to his funeral? Cause I sure as hell don't."

"Victor! This isn't the place for this," Aunt Pam said sitting beside him and tugging the bottom of Victor's suit jacket.

Brent balked and took a sidestep.

"C'mon Victor. Man, I didn't come here to start any trouble. I still love Valerie and I still love your family. I was hurt to hear that your father had passed," he said sadly.

Looking up at the 2 of them, I had a clear view for what was coming. Victor balled up his fist and brought it up into Brent's chin with force.

"You loved too many people in my family at the same time you bastard," Victor snarled.

Brent touched his chin and looked at Victor incredulously. I thought he was going to walk away, but to my surprise he threw a punch of his own and connected it with my brother's face. That's when all hell broke out. They scuffled throwing punches and grabbing at each other as funeral goers darted out of the way of their traveling brawl.

It took my uncle Jerry, my cousin Mark and 2 other male attendees to break it up; but not before the casket was bumped and reefs were trampled. Brent's tailored suit was torn around the collar, his chin was reddening, and his shiny bald head looked to be accompanied by a few new lumps. My brother's right eye was beginning to swell, and blood stained his white shirt with the blood from his busted lip.

The crowd was buzzing with people stating how disrespectful and tacky it was for them to be fighting as others straightened my daddy's casket back on the platform hovering it above the plot. I hadn't actually moved from my seat. Brent deserved every lick my brother gave him, and I was glad I was there to witness it live. I only wished that I could do the same to Vanessa, but she wasn't here, and I wasn't prepared.

You know, life is too short to live it on other people's terms and as of that moment, I was completely over caring what other people thought of me. There was definitely about to be some changes in my life, and I didn't care who was gonna like them. I dug through my purse for the dark tinted sunglasses I loved so much from the kiosk in the mall and stood up placing them on my face with a devious grin.

"Val are you okay?" Nicky asked rushing over to me through the crowd of people gathered around Brent and Victor who were now separated.

"I'm better than ever," I told her pushing her aside and strutting off towards the limo.

{ 14 }

Yasmin

My eyes were drenched with tears of remorse as I laid in the queen-sized bed in our spare bedroom, balled up in the fetal position. Everything had blown up in my face and now my life was in total shambles. Tamika knocked me out with one punch when Kamari told her what he'd witnessed and the bruises on my rib cage were evidence that she hadn't stopped there.

When I came to, a couple of people I didn't know from the HAIR TO THE THROWN staff were restraining her and Julian had me propped up in a stylist chair. I was in a total daze as I stood and tried to walk myself out of harm's way but nothing, including my legs seemed to be working right.

"Chile' sit your tail down in this chair. She knocked you into next week and your brain is still trying to bring you back. Here, drink you some water until your faculties are back working. You're safe as long as I'm standing here," he said handing me a styrofoam cup of water.

I drank the water wishing it was wine while she ranted savagely about what kind of back-stabbing, disloyal and barren bitch I was. I wanted to protest her calling me barren, but I knew that it would only add fuel to the fire, and I was already lucky to be breathing as it was.

When my father showed up, I knew there was no hope for me to come up with anything believable to save my own ass. It was too late.

Tamika or somebody had to have told him what happened because he wouldn't otherwise have been there.

The look of disappointment and bewilderment he gave me made my heart sink to the bottom of my feet. I had always been his pride and joy. Nothing like Tamika who never failed to disappoint with her multiple baby daddies, ghetto ways and ideas.

Now, I was going to be the new black sheep of the family. We hadn't even fully settled into the betrayal that Vanessa perpetrated on Valerie yet because it hadn't been a full week before my cat was tossed out of the bag. Tamika, being the messy bitch she is, promptly called Malik and let him know the news so when I got home, my workaholic, neglectful husband was suddenly home early.

When I walked in, he killed me with silence for the first 5 minutes but stalked me around the house until I asked him what his problem was. Of course, I didn't know at the time she'd called, but he laid into me like never before once he opened his mouth. He called me all kinds of sneaky, conniving, lying, hypocritical whores.

He read me up and down about all of the times he thought I was lying but tried to give me the benefit of the doubt and tried to get me to fess up to my activities the day of my carjacking but I didn't. What I did do, was sit in silence and let him speak. I never responded to anything he said. I just cried and stared like an emotional lunatic with no words to escape the asylum. Eventually, he exhausted himself cussing me out and stormed away from my worthless form sitting on the living room sofa Indian style.

We hadn't exchanged one word between us since that day and I hadn't been back to work. He got dressed and left each morning on schedule as if he was going to the office, but I wasn't really sure what he was doing after work since he hadn't been coming in until close to midnight. I wasn't in any position to question him; however, so I didn't. I just did what I was doing now. I cried myself to sleep.

Today they were burying my Uncle Vernon and my heart was truly heavy for his loss. When my dad was suffering through the loss of my mother, my uncle stepped up and made sure us girls were still okay. He was my dad's baby brother, but he was always there for my dad as much as my dad was for him. I knew my entire family would be there and that it would look odd if I wasn't as well, but I couldn't be.

I wanted to go as support for my daddy and to pay my last respects and to show my aunt and cousin's some love but, I couldn't bear to be in the same space with Tamika right now. Not only because she was too unpredictable, but because I knew there would be a lot of whispering about what happened between us. I was already ashamed of my actions and I didn't need anybody else to reiterate what I was already feeling. As it currently stood, no one in the family was speaking to me and when I reached out to my baby sis Nicky in hopes of explaining my side, she told me to 'call somebody who gives a damn.'

Tamika kicked him out of the house as soon as she got home and from the way Dwayne spoke to me on the phone that evening, he wasn't too distraught about it. Dwayne sent me a text message on Saturday asking me how me and the baby were. I texted him back that we were fine as far as I knew. I hadn't been to the doctor and I wasn't really sure which kind of doctor I was going to go to anymore. I was sure that I was going to keep this baby when I first found out about it but now, after just a taste of the backlash, I wasn't sure if I could handle it.

Tamika and Malik still didn't know about that aspect of Dwayne's and my affair and though Malik hadn't said it, I knew he was planning to divorce me. I know, I know, what did I expect right? But I truly thought that I could seamlessly sleep with another man until Malik and I worked out our issues. It wasn't the fact that Dwayne was Tamika's man that made him an option. It was the fact that he was a man other than my husband. We were supposed to go to counseling, and I thought that he and I would be even-Steven once it all came out in the wash.

My bladder was starting to feel like a reservoir filled to the brim, so I dragged myself from the bedroom and headed to the full bathroom at the end of the hallway. Malik startled me on his way out of it because

I wasn't even aware that he'd stayed home from work. Mourning my uncle's death had given me cause to imprison myself in the bedroom all morning and this was the first time I'd left it.

He stood in the doorway glaring at me, holding something in his hand that I couldn't make out until I got closer. My eyes bulged from its sockets and panic overtook my heart pace.

"So, when were you going to tell me?" he asked holding the EPT test I'd thrown in the trash days ago.

I was so tired of coming up with lies and trying to avoid whatever consequences that may come that I just decided to come clean with whatever he wanted to know. Just let the cards fall where they may, and I'd pick up whatever I could salvage later.

"I'm not sure if I ever was," I told him crossing my arms and embracing my shoulders apprehensively.

He stood barefoot, wearing his favorite old jogging pants and a Georgia State T-shirt with a blank expression that both made me nervous and frightened. His almond shaped eyes were mere vacant slits as he glanced down at the test and then back up to me.

"You aren't going to keep it?"

"I don't know. I haven't decided yet."

"So, it's his baby?" he asked icily.

I bit my bottom lip and nodded as my bladder screamed at me to go to the bathroom before I soiled my pajama bottoms.

"I really have to pee," I told Malik attempting to get past him.

"You slept with that low-life, drug-dealing, scumbag with no condom? You didn't even have the decency to protect yourself?" he grimaced scanning the hallway as though there were answers to his questions somewhere within it.

"Please Malik. I really have to pee," I begged trying to push the arm he'd placed on the frame which blocked my entry.

He coldly pivoted out of the way and I rushed in past him, dropping my bottoms quickly and relieving myself with a fervor. When I looked up, Malik was still standing in the doorway, glowering at me with a hateful look on his face.

"So all this time...you were demonizing me for having a few lunches and sharing a kiss with a woman I barely saw; meanwhile you were fucking your sister's son's father raw? Is that what I'm finding out?" he laughed maniacally launching the test at my face.

I dodged it just in time but fell off of the toilet for my efforts.

"Malik!" I cried out catching myself just in time to miss hurting myself on the tub beside it.

"You're a rotten bitch. You know that? I could've been living in the lap of luxury in D.C. right now if it wasn't for you. All of your fucking promises about the empire we were going to build together. The power couple we were going to be in Atlanta with our own personal injury firm. Oooh yeah. You were big on selling me dreams, weren't you? But when it came time to actually build on that dream, all you wanted to do was look pretty. I'm the one who works my ass off on these cases here. I'm the one keeping the team in line and making sure that our firm is profitable and that we've hired the right people. We were supposed to be doing that to-gether. You and me Yasmin. You and me!

Then as soon as you found out you might not be able to have kids, it's like that was it. You stopped sleeping with me regularly, you became preoccupied with your nephews, you started spending all of your time making sure you looked good...but not for me! Not for your own fucking husband who you claimed to love and cherish so much. Who you claimed to want to have a family with. So yes. I let myself get distracted by another woman. Yes! I sent some inappropriate texts and kissed her once. Once Yasmin! But did I ever...ever, sleep with another woman on you? No!"

The rage in his eyes was formidable causing me to quiver as I cleaned myself and pulled my pajama bottoms up to my waist.

"I... I'm sorry," I stammered tepidly leaning against the bathroom sink as I flushed and began to wash my hands.

I hoped that if I continued on normally, that he'd just leave me alone.

"How many times did you fuck him Yasmin?" he asked getting into my face just as I'd turned away from the sink.

When I didn't respond, he encroached even more upon me and glared into my fearful eyes with a flushed face.

"And so help me God if you just play that silent game that you've been playing, I will snap your neck where you stand," he barked.

"Maybe 5," I told him underestimating by at least half and hoping that would soften the blow.

He looked stunned and even stumbled back a little when I answered.

"Five!" He hollered.

I ran a hand over the top of my head and felt the pangs of uneasiness pulling at my chest.

"Wow. You scummy bitch," he said stalking off and leaving me with my thoughts.

I exhaled, happy that he was at least done with his interrogation for now, and dried my hands on the towel by the door. The spare bedroom I was staying in was on the first floor and just a few yards off of the kitchen. I chose that room instead of the others because I figured it would be the easiest to exit and enter without alerting him of my comings and goings. Not that I had come and gone much since everything came out though.

I walked gingerly back to my room with my thoughts on everything, feeling the worst I've ever felt in my life. Just as I was turning into the bedroom, I felt a sharp pain in my shoulder, then my back as I fell onto the carpet face down. Suddenly there was a heavy weight on my thighs and multiple agonizing blows reigned down onto my body.

"You-fucking-lying-bitch," Malik's maddened voice rang out through clenched teeth.

"You-fucking-lying-bitch!" he kept repeating.

I couldn't catch my breath to speak as I watched a pool of blood forming around me and felt his blows over and over and over...

{ 15 }

Amina

This was one of the saddest days of my life. Uncle Vernon was more than an uncle to me; he was a replacement father. Though my father is still alive, and I still see him on occasion, he's active when he feels like it and since I've been grown, that hasn't been too often. Hell, he didn't even drive up from Alabama to see me while I was in the hospital. Once he called and found out I wasn't going to die, he went on about his business with his new wife and 2 daughters.

It was Uncle Vernon who taught me how to drive. It was Uncle Vernon who laid down the law for my brother and I whenever my mom's strong-arming wasn't enough. I couldn't believe how suddenly he'd passed away, but at least I was lucky enough to have seen him in his last hours.

"You didn't eat much at the repast. Did you want me to stop and get something?" Donovan asked touching my hand affectionately.

He'd visited me every day at the hospital from that first time and we'd been getting closer than I ever expected. I'd been released without too many restrictions and I was actually walking fine, although my lower back did hurt me more often than not. I was controlling the pain with prescription drugs for now, but I was hopeful that they wouldn't be necessary for too much longer.

Donovan was more than helpful in my time of need though. He came over after he'd finished whatever he had going on for the day and made sure I had something to eat and had been taking care of myself as advised by my doctors. We shared a few passionate kisses on more than a few of his visits and I was tempted to try and skip straight to third base Friday night. If not for the sharp pain up my back that interrupted my grinding hips on his lap that night, I probably would've gotten what I wanted too.

I'd originally expected Valerie to be staying with me, so she was going to be my ride to the funeral and all proceedings. Apparently, she changed her mind about both though after our conversation about her and Maaco the other night. I mean, I didn't think it was that serious; our conversation I mean. But obviously she did because it got a little heated at one point and she was more than huffy about the subject. She even had the nerve to ask me if I had slept with Maaco before. Like really Boo? I can't be concerned about you unless I've slept with your man?

I just chalked up her oversensitivity to being a result of what Vanessa did to her, but clearly, she had taken my advice to her in a different spirit than it was given. I really didn't have a lot of time or energy to devote to her immaturity at the moment anyway, so I figured I'd give her time to cool off and we'd revisit whatever issues she had with me at that time. I mean, she did just lose her daddy and I wasn't oblivious to that. I'd never lost a parent, but I could only imagine the pain she felt since I'd felt much like Uncle Vernon was my own daddy.

"No, I'm good baby," I said before I could catch myself.

"Baby, huh? I like that. I'm your baby?" he asked with a wide grin turning onto the street where my subdivision was.

I blushed and turned my head to look outside so that my hair would block his view of my face.

"Yeah...I'm your baby," he chuckled causing me to join in.

Donovan had a charisma that I couldn't deny and with every day we got to know each other, I was feeling my heart open up to him. I was afraid to let him totally in though. I'd made the mistake of letting one man...or should I say boy...into my heart before and he crushed it into little pieces. I was very young at the time. Eighteen going on 25 if you'd asked me back then. I'd been totally head over heels for him and he hadn't only broken my heart, but my spirit as well. I vowed never to allow another man to do that for as long as I was able to breathe air. But now, I was almost contemplating it with Donovan.

"So, can I ask you something?" he questioned glancing at me as he drove.

"You can. I can't guarantee you that I will answer. But you can ask," I told him in total seriousness.

He frowned and had the nerve to actually look me up and down.

"Wow. Why're you so guarded? That's not the question I wanted to ask you but, now I want to know that too."

"Why don't we just start with whatever it was you wanted to ask me first. And then come back to the nosy and in my business question later," I told him with a grin.

He snickered again shaking his head.

"Girl, I swear. You are a trip. But anyway, I was gonna ask you if your brother is gay. Or maybe bi-sexual?"

I almost choked on my own spit in surprise at his question.

"What? No. Why would you even ask me something like that?" I retorted through coughs trying to clear my airway.

"Sorry. I didn't mean to shock you like that. I'm asking because of Dana. You said that's his girlfriend, right?"

"Yeah..." I nodded thinking that he wasn't making any sense.

"Well, at the repast, I accidentally walked in on...her...when I had to go to the bathroom. She forgot to lock the door and I didn't know anybody was in there, so I just opened it up."

"Okay. So how does that translate into my brother being gay or bi-sexual?"

"When I opened the door, she was peeing standing up and I ain't no homosexual or anything myself but, I ain't never seen a pussy that long in my life. Excuse my French," he said pulling up and parking his huge F150 truck into my driveway.

"What the hell! Are you serious?" I exclaimed covering my mouth.

I'd never had any inkling that my brother might be gay, and he'd been seeing Dana for nearly a year now. I didn't believe for a minute that he wasn't aware she was walking around with a dick in her pants. Especially if it was as big as Donovan led on.

"Umm...what the hell is that?" he said slowly gazing out of his windshield towards my house.

I'd have liked to faint when I saw the words GIVE ME BACK MY MONEY YOU SKANK BITCH HOOKER! spray painted on my garage door. My mouth almost came unhinged as I gawked out at the desecration some low life fuckbag decided to defame me with. Like who would even do this to me? I didn't owe anybody any money and I couldn't believe Jamie had anything to do with this because this was sooo not her style.

The police hadn't come up with any new leads yet, though I was told that they were going to see about reviewing surveillance tapes from some of the stores and police check points nearby. None of this made sense.

Donovan got out of his truck and walked around to help me out by simply lifting me into his arms and placing me down on my feet. He was so dramatic. Even when there were shenanigans ahead.

"Do you want me to come in with you?" he asked walking me up the winding pathway to my front door.

In hindsight, I wish that I had declined his offer.

"Yeah. I need to call the police about this crazy shit, and I want to make sure they haven't broken anything around my property so, if you can maybe just look around out back too for me?" I asked looking up into his worried eyes as I withdrew my keys from my bag and opened the door.

"Okay," he answered with a hand around my waist as we both entered.

Nothing looked out of place but the sounds of someone having loud sex echoed throughout the house. Donovan and I looked at each other perplexed since no one was supposed to be in my house and I hadn't given anyone but my mom the spare key to it.

"Who else has a key?" he asked quietly thinking on the same accord.

"Nobody," I replied feeling a bit frightful.

"Alright. Wait here," he told me pressing one hand gently to my chest and pulling out a handgun I'm wasn't familiar enough with to name.

He slowly ascended the staircase leading from the downstairs foyer to the bedrooms on the second floor.

Whomever was up there hadn't missed a beat as I heard a male voice say, "Yes Mistress! I have been very bad!"

My eyes could've burst from my head when I realized whose voice that was, and Donovan had already reached the top of the landing with his gun pointing towards the voices before I could even begin to move.

"Wait!" I yelled out trotting to the stairs.

"What the fuck?" he said bewildered lowering his gun with his face twisted into a frown.

He stood there dumbstruck, looking from me on my way up the stairs and towards the sound. There was a clear view from the top of the stairs into the master bedroom. A 55" flat-screen television hung on the wall parallel to the doorway, so if you were standing at the landing, you had a straight view of whatever was being watched on it.

Playing, live and in HD was a video of me with my hair in a tight bun on the top of my head, totally naked except for a leather waist cincher, spiked leather boots and holding a crystal tipped whip in one hand, and a leash hooked to the collar of a white man in the other. The man was howling in pain and pleasure as I dug the heel of my boot into his groin and twisted.

"Yes you have. Now eat this pussy!" I commanded yanking his leash viciously forcing him into a sitting position while my heel bore into him.

"Yes, Mistress please!" my prisoner begged as I opened my legs wide and drove his face into my awaiting snatch.

Donovan's eyes were not the windows to his soul. They were more like the windows to his revulsion as he surveyed me slowly, glanced back at the video and then placed his gun back into his waist.

"Excuse me," is all he said moving past me and descending the steps.

"Wait. I... I can explain what that is," I said helplessly.

He stopped and looked at me from the bottom of the steps.

"Yeah, you probably can but I don't think I want to hear it. I don't know what kind of shit you're involved in here with people shooting you, spray painting your garage and breaking in to play videos of you humiliating some guy but...this isn't anything I want to be tied to."

And on that note, he left my house, closing the door behind him. I leaned back against the wall and continued to watch the video with wet eyes. I hadn't known anyone was recording our sessions and now I was concerned about who would've cared. Everything I did was always discrete and that's the way my clients liked it.

Someone was really upset with me. And this was somehow related to Todd.

{ 16 }

Vanessa

I watched the melee ensuing on the burial grounds from a far and chuckled to myself. There goes Captain Save A Hoe defending his precious little Valerie again. My brother Victor was always ready and willing to take off a head when it came to his little sisters; but only one of us ever really needed him to do it.

I was surprised to see that Brent had even shown his face at my father's funeral under the circumstances, but I guess he thought it was a good idea. Brent's brother Dean probably couldn't make it on such short notice since he's a computer programmer for some company in Japan in addition to being an heir to the Lincoln fortune. Victor and Dean were like Fric and Frac whenever they were together, but I doubted Dean would've approved of the fisticuff sandwich he'd just fed his brother.

I didn't even know how Brent knew about my father's passing or where anything was at all to be honest with you. He surprised me by actually not calling me anymore after that night as I expected. Maybe he was telling the truth when he said that he loved Valerie that much. Shit, these days it seemed like everybody loved the bitch they were cheating on more than they loved the bitch they were cheating with.

The heels of my cherry Louboutin's were starting to dig into the grass as I stood on a hill in the distance wearing a simple knee length, black Ralph Lauren dress. Believe it or not, I'd intended to attend both the funeral services and the burial when I woke up this morning. But as I got dressed and thought about the way things went at the wake last night, the less I wanted to be around those squawking birds.

Valerie's phony ass sat around everyone trying to look as angelic as she could muster with her sad face and quiet ways. I'm not saying that she wasn't genuinely upset that my father died but...she just seemed to be milking the sympathy to the hilt. Every time I looked at her, she was gazing off into the distance and making people address her twice before she responded like she'd zoned out or something. Like bitch please! You know you heard them! She wasn't even my daddy's favorite.

Anyway, word had obviously gotten out about me fucking her lame ass man because I heard a few birds I didn't even know talking about it while they waited in the lobby to go into the room to view my dad's body. They were too busy running their beaks to see me getting a cup of lemonade from the table behind them, but I wasn't too busy to let them know I'd heard.

"No. The one with the black dress on is Valerie I'm telling you. The slutty one is wearing a skintight brown dress that looks like she bought it straight from Sluts-R-Us," A lanky skinny chick with tits the size of tic-tacs was telling 2 other homely looking bitches who looked like their biggest adventures included bible study and drinking communion.

"You are correct. That is Valerie. And no, I didn't get this fabulous Jason Wu dress from Sluts-R-Us, I got it off the rack at Neiman's. Anymore questions?" I asked with a condescending smile before sipping my lemonade and eyeballing every one of those crows.

"Oh. I'm sorry. We were just—," the homeliest bitch of the group began to say.

"No matter," I said waving her off and walking away.

I would never let such low-class, low-styled and low-leveled biddies disrupt my state of unbothered. I was here to pay my respects to my father, and they were not going to change that. Regardless, when I woke up this morning, I was in no mood to deal with anyone's fuckery and that included my mother who very politely asked me not to dress like a street walker for the services. She's never at a loss of insulting words for me; surprise, surprise.

I took my time getting dressed and made sure that my hair and make-up were done to perfection since I am a licensed cosmetologist, and headed off to the burial site where I thought I'd make a quick appearance and dash. When I arrived; however, I felt an overwhelming sense of sorrow that forced me to cry for no less than 15 minutes in my car.

Knowing that I'd ruined my make-up with my emotional outburst and no longer feeling up to being on display, I decided to park where a separate funeral was being held nearby for a stranger and simply watch my father's loved ones and the praise for his home-going from a far.

I couldn't believe that I'd actually forgotten to bring my sunglasses and; therefore, I was forced to watch with one hand hovering over my eyes to shield me from the bright sunlight. I enjoyed watching Brent get his ass handed to him. Even though I was a party to his cheating, he deserved what he got for being grimy enough to do it.

Valerie had on a similar dress to my Ralph Lauren's, but I couldn't tell who designed it from where I was and because she was sitting most of the time. I kind of missed talking to her like we had been at least once a week since she moved back to Atlanta from New York.

We still had our differences even then, but we'd been rebuilding the bond we lost when she went away to school and she had basically given me free reign of her closet. Originally, I wasn't impressed by the offer; but once I saw the wardrobe that Brent had provided her with and she told me how useless she found it, I was more than happy to help her get rid of them.

After the fight, the crowd seemed to dissipate and I'm sure my mother was pleased that the pastor had already said his prayers and service was over anyway by then. I watched curiously as Valerie sat there, watching them fight without one attempt at breaking them up.

In fact, she hadn't even uncrossed her legs to imply that she'd thought about it.

Getting my fill of everything, I turned and walked briskly back to my car getting inside and placing my handbag into the passenger's seat. I took a deep breath, contemplated my next move, then cranked up my car while shuffling through my ipod for the copy of my song that Faze gave me.

If you're man stacks his money, baby girl
And he wanna taste my honey, baby girl
You're about to be lonely, 'cause I'm rockin' your man's worrrrld
So keep him in the house, unless you wanna lose him
Keep runnin' your mouth, I ain't gonna refuse him
Cause when you're a boss-bitch-like-me-it's that eeeeeasyyyyy
To take your man
Take Take Take
Gimmie Gimmie Gimmie
Take Take Take
Gimmie Gimmie Gimmie

I made it to the repast in a good amount of time and to my delight, Valerie wasn't there at all. I didn't want to have to see her smug little face anymore today if I could help it and I figured she'd have had everyone fawning over her if she was. I spoke briefly to my mother, cousins, aunt and uncle; pretended to listen to other relatives and friends of the family's heartfelt condolences and got a little something to eat. An hour into it, I was looking at my watch with deliberation and calculating how much time it would take me to reach my destination if I left at that point.

I made sure not to draw attention to myself when I made my exit and strutted out the basement door past a few people coming in as I left. Thirty minutes later, I was pulling up to a quaint little jogging trail just off the beaten path in downtown Lawrenceville.

Thankfully, I kept a pair of running shoes in my backseat for times when the beautiful high-heel shoes I loved to wear so often, started to hurt my feet. Putting them on, I walked up the pathway for what was probably 10 minutes before I came upon a beautiful clearing that overlooked a bunch of trees, greenery and possibly parts of Stone Mountain Park below.

To my delight, the person I was looking for was up there doing yoga on a large mat with earbuds in her ears and no awareness of my presence. Idiot. Sometimes being popular isn't a good thing because people ask you a lot of questions about your life which allows everyone to know things they wouldn't otherwise know about you.

"So, what do you do to stay so fit?" some blog radio host had asked.

"Well, I don't do a whole lot actually. I'm not really an exercise kind of girl like some women are. I just want to stay healthy and toned. I only work out like twice a week really. Every Tuesday and Thursday, I jog up this little trail near Stone Mountain Park around 2 or 3 in the afternoon and do yoga overlooking nature. It's a place where I used to go with my ex all of the time but now that we're not together, it's become my place of tranquility. Get away from the noise of life you know?" Delia told the host.

"Oh my God. I've run up Stone Mountain before and girl that is no joke," she responded.

"Oh nooo! I'm not jogging up Stone Mountain. It's a trail near Stone Mountain Park. I think they call it Eve's Entrance or something like that. The place it overlooks is beautiful and I guess whomever named it that felt like it looked like it could've been the garden of Adam and Eve or something."

They both laughed and I remembered thinking how corny they sounded as I listened to the show I'd come to from a link Delia posted on her Twitter page. None of that was important to me back then, but it was certainly important to me today as I stood watching her in the downward standing dog position.

I allowed her to finish her set and laughed out loud when she nearly jumped out of her skin after turning to see me.

"What are you doing up here?" she asked with alarm as she withdrew the earbuds from her ears gaping at me with sweat rolling down her face.

"Paying you back bitch," I said coldly raising the .357 Magnum I'd been gripping in my hand toward her chest and pulling the trigger.

The shot made a booming sound as it left the chamber and fled towards her petite little body, nailing her dead center and sending her flailing backwards over the edge. I wasn't sure how far down the drop was, but I knew it was far enough to kill her if the gun shot hadn't, so I didn't even bother to go look in case there were people somewhere below.

Scurrying down the pathway back to my car, I glided my feet back and forth over each step the way an inline skater might move to muddy my footprints on the way down. Of course, it took me way longer to get down the path than it did up it, since I was performing cover-up moves upon exit, but I'm sure it would be well worth it to secure my future.

Brand took something from me...and I took something from him.

To be continued...

Enjoyed This Book?

Please leave a review on Amazon or Goodreads to share!

Other releases by K.F. Johnson:

BEHIND CLOSED DOORS: LOVE HURTS
LIAR'S BALL: BEHIND CLOSED DOORS 2
WHEN I'M BAD I'M BETTER
WHEN I'M BAD I'M BETTER 2
WHAT I'D DO FOR LOVE
WHAT I'D DO FOR LOVE 2
LOVE HURTS: SERIES COMPILATION
WHEN I'M BAD I'M BETTER FOREVER: SERIES COMPILATION
STABBED THIS CHRISTMAS: A NOVELLA

Join my mailing list and be the first to get sneak peeks, giveaways, contests, new release info, learn event appearances and more!
http://www.kfjohnsonbooks.com

"The Empress of romantic, murder, suspense", **K.F. Johnson** is a Queens, New York native residing in Atlanta, Georgia. As a child, habitually failing to make curfew before the streetlights lit, earned her numerous occasions on restriction where reading & writing became her main form of escape. Later, K.F continued to develop her talent while obtaining a B.A. in Psychology at Spelman College & acquiring an MBA. In 2012, she published her 1st book for her social media friends & family to see. To her delight, it went viral, repeatedly reaching #1 on Amazon's top 100 for its genre. Since then, K.F. has published multiple books, started One Ironwoman Publishing, been featured in magazines & nominated for numerous awards, both for her books & as an author. With her fan base cheering for more, this mother & wife has blossomed into a witty & cunning author, penning spicy, realistic & deadly tales of African American life to remember.

www.ingramcontent.com/pod-product-compliance
Lightning Source LLC
Chambersburg PA
CBHW071808190726
48292CB00008B/2764